"It isn't—" It  as far as she

"To hell with equality!" The chief troubleshooter at Benson Oil blasted her eardrums, and suddenly the fact that anyone could roar at her so made Joss exceedingly angry.

"That's typical of men like you!" she erupted.

"You know nothing at all about a man like me!" he rapped back, ignoring the angry sparks flashing in her dark brown eyes. "Nor will you!"

"I wouldn't want to," she flared, reading into his last three words all the confirmation she needed that she wouldn't be staying. And after having been so excited about this trip to Egypt, she felt angrier than ever.

A FIRST TIME
FOR EVERYTHING

Jessica Steele

Harlequin Books

TORONTO • NEW YORK • LONDON
AMSTERDAM • PARIS • SYDNEY • HAMBURG
STOCKHOLM • ATHENS • TOKYO • MILAN

Original hardcover edition published in 1990
by Mills & Boon Limited

ISBN 0-373-03126-2

Harlequin Romance first edition May 1991

A FIRST TIME FOR EVERYTHING

CHAPTER ONE

IF SHE were to be truthful, Joss owned, she didn't feel very much like going out that Monday evening. She could not have said why particularly it was that the Beacon Theatre Group had no appeal that February night, though, as she poured herself a second cup of coffee, she didn't think the dull and gloomy weather had very much to do with the way she was feeling.

Silently she sipped her coffee, and a few minutes later she carried her used dishes from her dining-room and through to her smart cream and pale green kitchen, knowing that she would go out. It wasn't in her nature to let anyone down, and Abby, her closest friend, was at present smitten with Fergus Perrott and, for some reason, seemed to need her along to boost her confidence.

Joss set about tackling her washing up, reflecting that Fergus had not asked Abby to go out with him yet, but that these new and frequent visits to the Beacon Theatre Group—an offshoot of the Beacon Oil Sports and Social Club—seemed to be paying dividends. She was sure she had seen a gleam of interest in Fergus's eyes last Friday as he'd watched Abby during rehearsals. All three of them worked for Beacon Oil at Beacon House, London—she and Abby both on the secretarial side, while Fergus worked in Personnel.

Thinking of last Friday, Joss pondered that she must have been feeling a bit like today's weather then—or maybe started to feel in the need of something more stimulating than her present job, for she had realised

5

that she had been only half joking when she'd asked
Fergus then if his department had been notified of any
interesting secretarial vacancies.

'Finding the Audit Department too dull?' he'd
queried.

'It—has its moments,' she'd replied, 'but it's not as
challenging as it once was.'

'There's nothing more challenging just now than a
transfer to Costing,' Fergus had told her.

'I think I'll stay where I am—"Costing" doesn't sound
very much different from "Auditing",' she had
answered, being unable to see anything likely to stimu-
late by the switch.

Leaving her neat and tidy kitchen, Joss went to get
ready to go and pick Abby up. They had known each
other for three years now. The whole time in fact since,
at twenty years old, Joss, with her feet well and truly
on the secretarial ladder, had started work at Beacon
Oil.

In an attempt to lift her glum spirits, Joss tried to
count her blessings. She had a good job—a very good
job, she reminded herself. True, she had worked exceedingly hard to get on, and as a reward for being in-
dustrious she had been promoted several times in her
three years at Beacon House. She now worked for Mr
Edwards, head of the Audit Department, and she knew
without false modesty that he thought well of her.

The work she did was of a confidential nature and
had, at one time, stretched her abilities. But, having
worked for Mr Edwards for a year now, she no longer
felt stretched.

A short while later she left her apartment, telling
herself that she must not allow herself to get discon-
tented. She was well paid for her labours; the high salary

Beacon Oil paid her made the expense of buying her small but smart flat and running a car just affordable.

She and Abby took it in turns to use their vehicles, and as Joss drove along to her friend's home she attempted to make herself believe that it was just 'February' that was making her feel so unsettled. Maybe everyone felt the way she did during the second month of the year. Somehow, though, she didn't feel convinced.

Joss had only joined the theatre group at Abby's bidding and, aware that she had no acting ability, she was quite pleased to sit sewing or whatever else was required while Abby and the rest of them got on with it.

'He's not here!' Abby's hushed but disappointed wail as they entered the hall they were allowed the use of brought Joss rapidly away from her own thoughts.

'Perhaps he's out the back somewhere,' she tried to cheer Abby, not seeing anything so special about Fergus Perrott herself, but sympathising with Abby, who clearly did.

'I'll bet he's not,' Abby said, looking to an outer door as if hoping that Fergus would walk through it.

As it turned out, Fergus was not there, but they were half an hour into rehearsals and Joss, acting as prompter, was about to give Abby a line she had missed when, glancing up, she suddenly saw that Abby had not so much forgotten her lines, as had had them taken momentarily out of her head by the sudden arrival of Fergus Perrott.

'Sorry I'm late, everyone,' he boomed, and excused himself, 'Had to work late.'

'Aren't we the busy one!' commented a man next to Joss whom she knew only as Larry.

Though she had to hide a smile she couldn't help but agree that, with all of them working for the same firm,

Fergus had made it sound rather as if his job was of more importance than anyone else's.

When a short while later there was a general break while the producer went into a huddle with Abby and a few of the others, Fergus came over to Joss and Larry moved away. Joss noted the considering look Fergus gave her, but she thought he was still out to impress when he said after a dramatic moment, 'Ah, Josslyn, are you still looking for a job you can get your teeth into—something that's a little different?'

About to tell him that she had changed her mind, she opened her mouth—then hesitated. Suddenly, as it registered that, although she was only ever called Joss, he had called her Josslyn, she realised that he must have taken a peep at her personnel file. If he was so busy that he had to work overtime, then he wouldn't have time to waste on checking her file, would he? Not unless, she perceived, he had some good reason to check on her and her capabilities and any other notes made on her record with the company over the last three years.

So, 'I could be,' she said after some moments of deciding that it didn't seem that he could be speaking purely for effect.

'I'm sure you will be when I tell you…' Fergus began, and soon had Joss looking at him wide-eyed and incredulous as he revealed how a telex had been received from Beacon House, Cairo, late that afternoon stating that one top grade secretary would be returning to England, and requesting that another top grade secretary be sent out immediately.

Joss's mind was on the instant a seething mass of questions, but since one of her most heartfelt desires had always been to see the Pyramids at Giza, which she knew was not so very far away from Cairo, all she could gasp was, 'Cairo! You're offering me a job in Egypt!'

'It's only a temporary job,' Fergus hastened to tell her, and went on to explain how delicate negotiations were going on in Egypt with regard to a contract for the refining of great quantities of crude oil. 'The present secretary out there must have gone down with a bug or something,' he continued, 'which reminds me, you'll have to check up with our medical department tomorrow about jabs and things you'll need before...'

'Just a minute!' Joss stopped him before he could go racing on, while at the same time she tried to hold down an inner and growing excitement at the very thought. 'How long's temporary—and what do I do afterwards?' Suddenly some of her excitement faded. It was all very well to go rushing off to the Middle East at this quite terrific opportunity, but what about when the temporary job was over? Since she had a sizeable mortgage on her flat she just couldn't dash off without giving a thought to how she could meet those monthly mortgage repayments when she got back.

Fergus, it seemed, had an answer for everything. 'Mr Edwards will welcome you back with open arms, you know he will,' he declared, and Joss's feeling of excitement started to soar again.

She went home that night with her head spinning from the question and answer session she'd had with Fergus, and let herself into her flat and went over everything in her mind again.

The contract which Fergus had spoken of must be almost agreed upon, she mused, because according to him her stint in Egypt would only be for a month or so.

Which, she reflected as she went into her kitchen to make herself a hot drink, was so much the better from her boss, Mr Edwards', point of view. She thought that perhaps he might not be very keen to let her go, but maybe he wouldn't mind so much if it was only for a month—an absence of not much more than her annual holiday really, when he would have had to get someone else to do her work.

She mustn't start thinking of it as a holiday, she brought herself up short, having had other things to spend her money on since going in for flat purchasing, and a holiday being out of the question. Pulling her thoughts away from anything remotely connected with holidays, and burying such thoughts of how at last she was going to have the chance to see the fantastic, stupendous, mind-boggling Pyramids of Cheops, Chephren and Mycerinus, Joss tried for calm.

For a moment, several moments in fact, she had been uncertain that Fergus had the power to offer her the temporary job in Cairo. He was fairly high up the Personnel tree, she knew that, but the doubt had niggled so that she just had to ask, as tactfully as she could, 'Er—has Mr Grazier sanctioned your offering me this...'

She realised that perhaps she hadn't been as tactful as she had hoped when Fergus got on his dignity and told her grandly, 'As it happens, Mr Grazier is at present sunning himself somewhere in India—in his absence I have full charge of the office.'

'He's on holiday?' she queried, and found that she had deflected his hurt pride when he replied that his boss always chose to depart from England's shores in February, and then went on to tell her to bring her passport into the office with her tomorrow because she would have to see about getting a visa.

Joss went to bed that night still trying to keep a lid on her excitement. Nothing had been settled yet, she tried to remind herself. Fergus had told her not to mention anything to Mr Edwards tomorrow until she had heard from him—which had again made her wonder if Fergus had as much clout as he would have her believe. She recalled how he had said that the telex had been received late that afternoon, and could not help but wonder then if his telling her to hang fire meant that Fergus had to first convince someone else in his office that she was the right person to go.

Suddenly then she became a little proud of herself. Why shouldn't she go? Beacon Oil were a company that worked worldwide. Staff, secretaries, were often being sent all over the globe—as in the case of the secretary who was returning from Cairo—so why not her!

She felt too excited to be ready to close her eyes, and a whole range of thoughts had gone through her head before Josslyn eventually went to sleep. Her thoughts had grown hazy as sleep claimed her, but one of her last waking thoughts was to wonder if maybe Fergus was keen for her to have the job out of some wish to impress Abby with the power of his position, or perhaps—since from where he stood it must seem that she and Abby were inseparable, for they did most things together—if he was anxious to have her out of the way in order to have a clear field with Abby.

That same thought was in Joss's head as she sat in her office the following morning. She was certain, having caught the way in which Fergus looked at Abby, that he was interested in her friend. And although, on the face of it, it didn't seem possible that a man of such self-importance should be backward about asking Abby for a date, Joss was prepared to consider that her theory might be right.

'Good morning, Joss,' Mr Edwards, tall, beaky and fatherly, greeted her when he came in, and Joss was suddenly overwhelmed by a feeling of guilt.

'Good morning, Mr Edwards,' she replied, and badly wanted to tell him right then about her discussion with Fergus last night. Just in time, however, she remembered that Fergus had told her not to mention anything to Mr Edwards yet.

An hour later she was beginning to think that it was just as well she hadn't said anything to her boss—the way things were looking, there was nothing *to* tell him! Five minutes later, as she began to realise that it looked as though the temporary Egyptian job had gone to some other secretary, she began to feel a shade annoyed. She was as well qualified as most, and she must be jolly good at her job—or why else would she be holding down the responsible job she had now?

A minute afterwards, though, her phone rang, and suddenly, as Fergus Perrott said, 'You'd better see about getting your visa,' her annoyance abruptly vanished.

'You're . . . I'm going?'

'Didn't I promise you the job?' he answered smugly. But by then Joss didn't care how smug he sounded; she was going—going to Egypt! She was going—to see the Pyramids!

In actual fact her departure for Cairo was not as immediate as had been requested. Apart from her visa application and other formalities to attend to, she had to present herself for the various vaccinations thought advisable.

But it was someone in Personnel, however, who acquainted Mr Edwards with the fact that his secretary was being sent on loan to Egypt. They must have phoned through at the same time that she was speaking with Fergus, Joss realised—and have done their job most tactfully—for her boss did not seem too badly put out when, as she put down her phone after noting Fergus's lengthy instructions, Mr Edwards came into her office from his own.

'What's this I've just heard about you going to Egypt on some top priority, highly confidential matter?' he asked without preamble.

'Do you mind very much?' she asked him quietly.

'Yes,' he said severely, though he added, 'But as long as it's only temporary I'll do nothing to block you going.'

'I'll be back before you've noticed I've gone,' she promised, then set about doing the hundred and one things that suddenly presented themselves as most urgent.

By the time all formalities had been completed and her temporary successor initiated, the rest of the week had gone by. With arrangements made for her to fly out to Cairo on the following Monday, Joss spent the weekend with her parents at their home in Eastbourne and returned to London after lunch on Sunday to pack everything she had made ready in the evenings during the week.

The excitement that had been part and parcel of her since Fergus's phone call last Tuesday spiralled as her plane took off on Monday, churning away inside her throughout the flight.

None of that excitement had diminished when, having put her watch forward by two hours, she landed in Cairo a little after half past four that afternoon. By the time she had claimed her luggage and passed through passport control, it was nearing five, and Joss looked about for whoever had been sent to meet her.

It took all of five minutes as the arrival area emptied for it to dawn on her that whoever had been sent to meet her was late. When another ten minutes went by and no one had turned up, she found herself in something of a dilemma. What if the person who had been instructed to meet her had forgotten—or, worse, had been involved in an accident? It had gone five now and she had no idea if the Cairo office worked a nine-to-five day, but, as she saw it then, she considered that she'd be best employed in somehow getting to Beacon House with all speed.

She had no trouble in locating a taxi when she left the airport building, but had more trouble in getting the taxi-driver to take his eyes off her long ash-blonde hair.

'Can you take me to Beacon House, Cairo?' she asked him when she did gain his full attention and kept her fingers crossed that he could understand English.

To her relief he could, and not only that, but he seemed to know straight away where Beacon House was. With her luggage swiftly stowed away, the driver set off, with Joss hoping with all she had that she would not find the office closed when she got there.

If the worst came to the worst she could always book into a hotel overnight, she made contingency plans—though she prayed that it wouldn't come to that, and closed her mind to the possibility that February could be the height of the tourist season with all hotels fully booked.

Having decided what her plan of campaign must be, she took a moment out to notice the traffic. Horrendous was putting it mildly! As far as she could tell, traffic drove on the right, but with the proviso, or so it seemed, that one overtook on whichever side there appeared to be a gap. Her heart went into her mouth when it seemed to her that her driver took his taxi much too close to a man sitting astride a donkey which was taking a stroll down the main road. The donkey was unharmed, however, and as she twisted to look back to check, she saw that as well as being unharmed, the animal seemed oblivious to the traffic and the incessant blaring of car horns that went with it.

She forgot all about the donkey, however, when, facing the front again, she noticed that the taxi was slowing down. Her heart picked up a few agitated beats when the driver finally stopped outside a smart-looking glass-fronted building. Peering from the window of the taxi, she read with relief the embossed 'BEACON HOUSE' over the doorway, and turned back, intending to ask the driver to wait while she checked if there was anyone about— what she didn't need, if the office was closed, was to go wandering the streets of Cairo with her heavy suitcase looking for a hotel.

But the driver was already out of the car, she saw, and was round the back extracting her luggage, so swiftly she left the vehicle too, and went quickly to test the door of Beacon House. To her utmost relief, it yielded. She went in—the taxi-driver followed.

A man somewhere in his late twenties and of medium height got to his feet as she went further inside. 'Do you speak English?' she asked him.

Her relief was total when, with just a hint of a London accent, he replied, 'Most of the time—who,' he added admiringly, 'are you?'

But Joss had other things on her mind just then than embarking on flirty repartee with this representative of Beacon Oil who obviously liked what he saw.

'I'm the replacement secretary from England,' she told him, 'I've just come from the airport.' She saw that, for all he appeared to look momentarily stunned, he had a quick standard of recovery. For in no time he had taken her large suitcase from the taxi-driver and—somewhat to her amazement—had what seemed to her to be an argument with him in Arabic, and, all before she had got herself completely together, he had paid her taxi fare and had sent the driver on his way.

'Rule number one,' he told her as he turned back to her, 'never pay the first price they ask. In actual fact,' he went on knowledgeably, 'you should have agreed the fare before you got into his taxi.'

'How much do I owe you?' Joss asked him.

'Forget it, I'll claim it on expenses,' he told her. Then, smiling a welcoming smile, 'I'm Baz Barton.' He held out his hand.

'Joss Harding,' she told him, shaking hands, and went on, 'I wasn't quite sure what to do when there was no one at the airport to meet me...' She broke off as a door leading into another office opened and another man of about the same age and stature as Baz Barton—clearly attracted by the sound of voices—came through.

'Look what we have here,' Baz Barton addressed the other man in tones that hinted, to Joss's mind, that he was surprised to see her there at all! 'This is Joss Harding from Beacon, London,' Baz went on, 'Joss, the manager of Beacon, Cairo, Malcolm Cooper.'

'Glad to know you, Joss,' said Malcolm, extending his right hand.

'Weren't you expecting me?' she questioned, the question seeming to her to be one needing to be asked if one linked the manager's quickly hidden look of surprise with the fact that no one had been at the airport to meet her, not to mention that certain something in Baz Barton's tone just now.

'Last week we were expecting—er—a replacement,' Malcolm replied. 'London should have let us...' He broke off then, smiling cheerfully. 'But you're here now—and welcome. Now,' he swiftly got his thoughts together, 'when did you last eat?'

His question was not one she had been expecting, but as the excitement she had nursed over the hours settled down, she only then realised that she felt hungry.

'I had a meal on the plane,' she replied.

'Which was hours ago. Baz and I were going to have a bite any time now. Leave your case here,' he decided, and, checking his watch, he turned to Baz Barton and remarked, 'He won't be here for a couple of hours yet; we might as well go now.'

They were all three sitting in the coffee bar of a nearby hotel, and Joss was tucking into a cheese omelette that came complete with chips, before she learned more of the 'he' who was expected some time after two hours had passed.

As yet, she had no idea where she would lay her head that night, but she was in the company of two of her fellow countrymen, both of whom she assumed knew Cairo well from the way they were instructing her on the various do's and don'ts. Apparently, while it was 'not done' to try and get a reduced price in any of the recognised stores, it most definitely was 'done' to haggle in the bazaars. More, it seemed one risked spoiling the market traders' enjoyment if one did not enter the 'haggling' game.

With her anxieties abated now that she had traced the two Beacon 'locals', Joss, who—no matter how she was feeling inside—had earned a reputation for being un-flappable, accepted that where she would lay her head that night was no immediate cause for concern. Malcolm, she realised, must be the man who was negotiating the contract for the refining of crude oil, so she would be working for him.

It was on the tip of her tongue to ask him what particular bug had laid his previous secretary so low that she had had to return home—he had already warned her about the water, stressing that she must not even clean her teeth with it. Suddenly, though, Baz Barton was voicing the opinion that it was a good job she had arrived that day rather than tomorrow.

'Why particularly?' she asked.

'Because we normally shut up shop at five and leave work for the day,' he replied.

Joss was about to refer in passing to her contingency plan of taking herself off to a hotel for the night if need be—and of presenting herself at Beacon House in the morning—when a stray strand of curiosity stirred.

'You had some particular reason for not closing the office at five tonight?' she queried.

'Too true,' Malcolm took up. 'Thane Addison rang just before you arrived...'

'Thane Addison!' Joss exclaimed. His name was legend back at Beacon House, London. She had never met him, of course, but she knew his name well enough. According to popular report, as well as having a seat on the board of Beacon Oil, Mr Thane Never-still-a-minute Addison was Beacon's chief anywhere-in-the-world troubleshooter. 'Is Thane Addison here—in Egypt?' she questioned, and started to feel quite excited again. Especially when she heard Malcolm's reply.

'Not only is he in Egypt,' he told her, 'but he's on his way to Cairo right at this very moment.'

'Wh-where's he coming from?' Joss asked when she had got her breath back.

'Alexandria,' she was told, and, as the meal ended, she learned that the reason why both Malcolm and Baz had still been on the premises when she had arrived was that Thane Addison had phoned to say he was on his way to sign some papers they had ready for him. While they waited they had decided to have a bite to eat nearby, after which they would return and be back at the office for when he arrived.

Joss returned to the office with them. By that time all daylight had gone and she was beginning to feel that she wouldn't mind at all if someone gave her some kind of a lead as to where she would be kicking off her shoes that night. But for the moment she decided not to say anything to Malcolm that might be of a problem nature—not that she could think of her overnight accommodation as being anything of a problem. But quite clearly Malcolm, as well as Baz, seemed slightly nervous of Mr Addison's visit—they could sort it all out when he had gone.

It was nearing eight o'clock that night when, with all three of them waiting in the outer office, Malcolm, who had been watching the window, suddenly shot to his feet. 'He's here!' he said, and as suddenly, Baz Barton had shot to his feet too.

It must have been infectious, Joss realised a moment later, because as the door into the outer office was thrust open she discovered that she was on her feet too. She acknowledged then that she was quite excited at the thought of meeting the much-talked-of Mr Thane Addison in person.

Within a very short while of the tall, broad-shouldered, fair-haired man's entering the room, however, Joss was no longer sure about how she felt. Thane Addison seemed to be somewhere around thirty-seven, she would have said, had an air of knowing what everything was about—and had a pair of piercing grey eyes which, she was soon to learn, never missed a thing.

He came in, briefcase in hand, nodded to both Malcolm and Baz, spotted her—and her large suitcase nearby—and stopped dead. Then, without waiting for either of the other two men to perform the introduction but—even as she formed the idea that he had quickly assessed who she was—fixing those piercing grey eyes on her wide brown ones, he was demanding coldly, 'Who the devil are you?'

Joss was unused to anyone talking to her in such a fashion, but she hadn't come all this way to have a slanging match on landing with one of the company's board members. So she drew her unflappable self out of hiding, and in clear tones told him formally, 'My name's Josslyn Harding. I'm the replacement for the secretary who returned to England last . . .'

'The hell you are!' he cut rudely across what she was saying. And, while she stared at him and had the hardest work to remain outwardly unflappable, he snarled, 'You're saying that they've disregarded my instructions entirely, and sent you as Paula Ingram's replacement!'

'I rather think,' Joss replied, as every muscle in her body tensed, 'that they have.'

That was not all she thought, for as his words 'my instructions' penetrated, all her excitement rapidly disappeared. All at once, even though she found the thought too incredible, she was gaining the most definite view that she had made a mistake in thinking that she had been sent here to work as Malcolm Cooper's temporary secretary. Suddenly, as she stared into the hostile eyes of Thane Addison, she received the most definite vibes that he was to be her new temporary boss!

Though, as cold steely eyes pierced into her, she suddenly had the most concrete feeling that the job wouldn't even last as long as temporary. Because, as she stared back at him, it startlingly began to dawn on her that, if she was reading the signs correctly, Thane Addison would soon be ordering her back to England—on the very next plane!

CHAPTER TWO

FOR how long she and Thane Addison continued to stare at each other, Joss couldn't have said. So taken aback was she by him, by his manner, and by the fact that it seemed that he was the man she had been sent to Egypt to work for, that she was oblivious to the fact that there were spectators present.

Thane Addison had not forgotten, however, though she was still staring into his cold steely eyes when he flicked his glance to the two witnesses, then commanded her harshly, 'Follow me!' In the next moment, without a by-your-leave to the Cairo office manager, he turned about and without checking to see if she was 'following' went striding into Malcolm Cooper's office.

It was Joss who closed the door after them. If he had anything tough to say, and from the look of him she guessed that he had, then she thought she would prefer not to have an audience.

'Who assigned you to this job?' he rapped before her fingers had time to leave the door handle.

'Fergus—Fergus Perrott,' she replied and, too late, she saw as his eyes narrowed that it might have been better had she replied 'Personnel'. 'He works in Personnel,' she added, hoping to make things better, but only to discover that—nobody getting up earlier in the morning than this man, apparently—she had only made things worse.

'This Perrott—he's a personal friend?' Thane Addison charged, and for the first time in her life Joss felt backed into a corner. She did not like the feeling.

'Yes,' she told the tall and aggressive-chinned man opposite her. 'But I got the job on merit, not through the "old pals" network.'

'You're sure about that?' he rapped.

Briefly Joss hesitated, and too late realised that the sharp-eyed man she stood before had noted that hesitation—even if she did rapidly follow it up with a positive, 'Yes, I am.'

'You were called to the Personnel department, were you?' he demanded, and Joss saw that here was a man who would get any truth out of you whether you wanted to reveal the exact circumstances or not.

'Does it matter?' she queried, her unflappable front sorely in danger of slipping. 'Fergus Perrott might have told me of the temporary vacancy because he and I were in each other's company that evening after the telex had come through...' Oh grief, she thought, realising that she was making it sound even worse than ever. 'But I've worked at Beacon House, London, for three years now, and he must have checked my personnel file and have seen that...' this was no time to be modest '...that I'm no slouch when it comes to being an efficient confidential secretary.'

For perhaps two seconds Thane Addison stared coldly at her tall trim self, then, rocking back slightly on his heels, he questioned, 'Does your super-efficiency include your being fluent in Arabic?'

'I... No... I...' she broke off, and knew positively that she would be going home on the next plane. 'Fergus didn't say...' she broke off as she realised she wasn't doing Fergus any favours—not that after this he deserved any, if what this man had said was true—and she supposed it was. 'I didn't know you'd asked for an Arabic speaker,' she said lamely, and started to feel a shade indignant suddenly as it occurred to her that, in the limited time available, Fergus would have been hard put to it to find a 'fluent' *and* 'top grade' secretary!

'Nor did he tell you, obviously, that I more specifically stated that I wanted a male secretary!' Thane Addison grunted, chips of ice glistening in his eyes.

'There must have been some mix-up over the telex,' Joss replied and, as she realised that she could say goodbye to the job for sure now, her indignation got the better of her. 'Though I think I should mention—in case it's some time since you last worked in Great Britain— that there's such a thing as the Sex Equality Act in force now. It isn't...' It was as far as she got.

'To hell with equality!' The chief troubleshooter at Beacon Oil blasted her eardrums, and suddenly the fact that anyone could roar at her so made Joss exceedingly angry.

'That's typical of men like you!' she erupted.

'You know nothing at all about a man like me!' he rapped back, ignoring the angry sparks flashing in her dark brown eyes. 'Nor will you!'

'I wouldn't want to!' she flared, reading into his last three words all the confirmation she needed that she wouldn't be staying. And, after having been so excited about this trip, she felt angrier than ever. 'It's no wonder to me at all,' she stormed on heatedly, 'that—that...' what was the woman's name? Paula Ingram, that was it. '...that Paula Ingram had to return home sick. The only wonder...'

'For your information,' he sliced thunderously through what she was saying, 'Paula Ingram didn't return to England because she was sick, but because I sent her packing when she went all female on me and let her emotions get in the way of her work.'

Joss was not sure that her mouth did not fall open as the import of what he had just said struck her. 'You *sent* her home?' she queried, her fury with him negated by her surprise. 'You—*dismissed* her!'

'That's what I said,' he bit back toughly.

'B-because of her—emotions?' Joss still couldn't quite believe what she was hearing.

'I was called in when negotiations with the Osiris Corporation started to foul up. I came to work—so did she,' he grunted, and tossed at her bluntly, 'The job I'm here to do is proving sticky enough without my having to contend with some female with over-active hormones!'

'Over-active hormones!' Joss repeated in astonishment.

'I don't know how else you'd describe some woman—without the least encouragement from me—taking it upon herself to declare her undying love,' he told her curtly.

'For you?' she exclaimed, and as her eyes went saucer-wide in her face, 'Paula Ingram told you she loved you?' she asked, aghast.

'And if you're half the confidential secretary you say you are, you won't repeat that outside of this room,' he pronounced, his jaw jutting at an aggressive angle again.

'As if I w...' Suddenly Joss halted. Was she imagining it or, despite her losing her temper, despite what had been said, was there an intimation there that he was going to allow her to stay to complete the job she had been sent to do?

'You hadn't better!' he did not wait for her to finish before threatening. 'Nor, if you've any interest in furthering your career with Beacon Oil, will you let your hormones get out of control while you're working for me!'

'My godfathers!' Joss snapped, her normally even temper on the the rampage again. 'I'd as soon...'

'I've enough problems in ironing out the difficulties which Yazid Rashwan daily puts in my path,' he strode straight over her eruption, 'without having to take time out to discipline another member of staff who takes it into her head to go all female on me.'

Joss had no idea at all who Yazid Rashwan was, but just then she was unconcerned with who he was. More particularly, she was staring at Thane Addison in absolute incredulity. The man was warning her off! This man was laying on the line that she was not to get any romantic ideas about him and was *actually warning her off*!

'I assure you, Mr Addison...' she began when she had her breath back. But again she broke off. Somehow, where once she had been certain she would be taking the next plane to England, she now somehow knew that—providing of course that she behaved herself—she was going to be allowed to stay. A swift memory of how she had always wanted to see the Pyramids at Giza sprang to her mind and, as a familiar dart of excitement speared her, she knew that—despite having to work for this brute of a man—she wanted to stay.

'Yes?' he queried curtly, having been watching her the whole of the time.

His query reminded her that she hadn't yet told him what she was assuring him of. 'I assure you,' she repeated, and unknowingly tilted her head a proud fraction, as she added, 'that oil would turn to water before you'd have need to discipline *me* on *that* score.'

Had she hoped to dent his ego a little, then Joss was disappointed. For he was singularly unimpressed as he grunted, 'Huh!' and then commanded her abruptly, 'Go and wait in the outer office.' She was on the way to the door when he added, 'Tell Cooper to come in.'

I wonder if he's ever heard of the world 'please', Joss thought briefly, but by then she was telling Malcolm, 'Mr Addison would like to see you,' and Malcolm was wasting no time in getting to what was his own office.

'Perhaps,' Baz Barton said as the door closed on the two, 'I should have mentioned that Mr Addison wanted a male to replace Paula Ingram.'

'It's not important,' Joss swiftly slipped into her unflappable role to reply, though she was sufficiently curious to tack on, 'I didn't know that anyone else was aware of Mr Addison's request, though.'

'The telex went from here,' Baz explained.

'I see,' Joss smiled, and because she had one or two things to think about, yet sensed that Baz wanted to talk, she asked, 'Is there somewhere I can wash my hands?'

Having made her escape, she went over her interview with Thane Addison a second time. Very soon she was fuming again. Instant dismissal, to her mind, was one dickens of a way to discipline somebody! Poor Paula Ingram!

A few minutes later, though, Joss wasn't so sure that she felt so very sorry for Paula Ingram. To hear Thane Addison tell it, he had given the woman no encouragement whatsoever. So what sort of female, unencouraged, would suddenly declare undying love?

On thinking about it, though, Joss realised that she had been in an office environment for long enough to know that some women did occasionally imagine—entirely uninvited—that they were in love with a boss who sometimes praised them for a job well done. Against that, though—Thane Addison! And what praise would he give? He didn't even know how to say 'please'!

Joss left the cloakroom having decided that she would probably work herself to a frazzle before Thane Addison would praise anything she did. It was only because he must by now be fairly desperate for a secretary that he had agreed to her staying at all, she suddenly realised. It was for certain that, while she didn't like him, he reciprocated that feeling of dislike in full measure.

All at once, though, it came to Joss that he didn't have to like her, did he? Only then did it dawn on her that the only reason he had not sent her packing was that—in a business capacity—he needed her. To wait for Beacon House, London, to send another secretary out—a male one this time—could take all of another week. Which meant that Thane Addison would use her, because it was expedient to do so.

At that point in her thinking Joss realised that she felt tired and weary and that she was grateful for the chair which Baz Barton indicated she should take while they waited for Thane Addison and Malcolm Cooper to finish their business in the other office.

'How was London looking when you left?' Baz enquired idly as they waited.

London, she thought wistfully, and tried to remember why she had been so eager to leave it. The Pyramids, she recalled, and smiled at Baz as she asked him, 'How long is it since you were there?'

She did not get to hear his answer, because just then the door to Malcolm Cooper's office opened and, briefcase in hand, Thane Addison came striding through. Joss saw his sharp glance go from her curving mouth and to Baz, then back grimly to her. She gained a clear impression from his grim look that she had just earned herself another black mark; the first for daring to be of the female sex, the second because he quite clearly thought she was passing the waiting time in having a light flirtation with Baz Barton.

'Come with me!' he commanded her curtly and, without a break in his stride, he headed for the outer door.

Both Malcolm and Baz dived to hand her her case, but Joss got to it first. Thane Addison was by then going out through the door, and, with no time to wish the other two individual goodnights, Joss called, 'See you!' and as fast as she could considering her handicap, with Baz holding the door open for her, she hurried after the man she was beginning to hate rather than merely dislike.

After a minute or so of charging after his departing back, however, she felt her temper start to fray and—working overtime that day—it came out yet again. Abruptly she stopped. Abruptly she thumped her case down and decided, damn him, enough was enough.

Her show of defiance proved to be brief, though, because just then the man up in front reached a sleek dark car that was obviously his, and he too stopped. Joss picked up her case again, and by the time she got to him he had the car door unlocked and was in the act of opening up the boot.

Unspeaking, he stretched out a hand and, as if it weighed nothing, took her heavy case from her and placed it in the rear compartment.

'Where are we going?' Joss questioned when after closing the boot he remembered such courtesies as to go and open the passenger door for her.

'Alexandria!' he clipped, and left her staring after him stunned as, plainly believing that she was big enough to get into the car by herself, he left her and went round to the driver's door.

Alexandria! Getting herself a little together, she seated herself in the passenger seat, and closed the door. By that time Thane Addison was in his car and was setting it in motion, and Joss saw that even at this time of night—and by then it was around eight-thirty—the traffic was still crazy.

She waited only to observe that he was not turning a hair as he drove into the car-horn-blaring nightmare of motorised confusion, and decided that he appeared to be more than capable of coping with anything, and that her questions were not likely to interfere with his driving. 'How far is Alexandria?' she asked coolly, having no idea if that city lay a few miles around the next bend or how far away it lay.

'About two hundred kilometres,' he deigned to toss in her direction.

Two hundred kilometres! Joss swallowed down the exclamation and by quickly dividing by eight and multiplying by five she reached the calculation that Alexandria was a hundred and twenty-five miles distant! It could take all of three or four hours to get there!

Wondering if she was ever going to get to bed that night, she choked back her astonishment that, unbelievably, she was now on her way to Alexandria and, striving hard to retain a cool note she commented evenly, 'I rather thought I'd be working in Cairo.'

'Complaining already?' Thane Addison grunted, and awakened in Joss latent ear-boxing tendencies.

She had far more control than to give in to the urge to set about him, however, though his—in her view— uncalled-for nasty remark left her deciding that she'd die sooner than volunteer another comment to the swine of a man. Lord, who could love such a man? Paula Ingram must be weak in the head!

For quite some while Joss silently fumed about the man she had the misfortune to be sitting next to, then gradually her anger subsided. Then it was that she noticed that they had left Cairo behind and were now speeding over a main toll road and that, apart from a parallel tarmacked road for traffic going in the opposite direction, they seemed to be driving through the desert.

Excitement flared up in her again, and momentarily vanquished any tiredness caused by being up at the crack of dawn and the ensuing weariness brought on by waiting at the airport, by travelling, and by waiting at Beacon House in Cairo. She was here! She was actually in Egypt! And she didn't care a button about the pig of a man driving this car. She was good at her job—and she would jolly well show him!

How Thane Addison had crept back into her thoughts again, she wasn't quite sure. But she pushed him out again and for some miles concentrated on the never-ending succession of large advertising hoardings to be seen in the cars' headlights.

Soon, however, the flashing billboards started to have a hypnotic effect and gradually her eyes began to close. Abruptly Joss jerked herself awake. But when tiredness joined forces with the weariness from her trials and tribulations of that day, suddenly the battle to keep awake was lost.

She drifted to the surface to discover that the car had stopped. She opened her eyes, and as she came fully awake, was instantly horrified to discover that she had either slipped or moved sideways in her sleep, and that her head was now resting, in supreme comfort—on Thane Addison's manly shoulder!

In the next split second she was sitting bolt upright and rapidly trying to decide if she should apologise for using him as a pillow, while wondering—in the light of Paula Ingram's so recently throwing herself at him—if he thought she was of the same inclination. As she got herself more of a piece, however, Joss's streak of unflappability began to stand her in good stead, so that she did not apologise but thought, by showing him some degree of coolness, to let him know that she'd as soon fall off the top of the highest Pyramid as fall for him.

So 'Where are we?' she questioned him aloofly, and very nearly lost all sign of being cool when, his lofty manner knocking hers sideways, he threw over his shoulder as he got out of the car,

'My apartment.'

Joss got out of the car too, and went to join him at the boot, from where he was extracting his briefcase and her suitcase.

'Why?' she questioned.

'What do you mean, why?' he challenged, and when she just stood and stared at him, he gave her an irritated look, then, his voice more an aggressive snarl than anything, 'It's gone eleven, and this is where I live,' he stated bluntly, 'and if you think I'm toting you around Alexandria trying to check you into a hotel at this time of night, then do *you* have another think coming!'

'You're saying that I'm staying *here*?' Joss questioned, but with her case in his grip he was already locking up the boot.

She did not thank him that, not bothering to reply, he led the way into the apartment block. To carry her case was the least he could do, in her opinion. She was glad, though, that from what he *had* said she was able to glean the knowledge that he knew she would have preferred a hotel to his hospitality.

Though why a man who'd had the gall to warn her off should then bring her to his apartment was beyond her. Most odd, she thought as they entered the building, and then wondered—was it odd, though? Perhaps she wasn't as wide awake as she had thought, but somehow, even to her weary self, it seemed quite credible that this swine who was now greeting the concierge in Arabic

'*Masa'il kher*, Mustapha,' could be putting her to some kind of test.

Well, he needn't worry himself that she might try to join him in his bed that night, she thought in disgust, and strangely, as she went up some marble steps with him, she heard herself asking, 'Is there a Mrs Addison?'

They had reached a first-floor landing and he was inserting a key into one of the doors before 'I've a mother—in England,' he drawled arrogantly.

'I won't ask about your father,' Joss muttered, needled by his high-and-mighty arrogance, and so fed up with him and his manner suddenly—even if he was her boss—that she was feeling just scratchy enough not to care whether he had heard or whether he hadn't.

He had heard, though. But although she would not have been surprised to have something short, pithy and painful hurled back at her for her intimation that she doubted that he had ever had a father, suddenly, and to her utter amazement, she saw his rather well-shaped lips twitch.

She was still not quite believing that she had somehow reached his sense of humour when, his mouth setting in firm lines, all sign of his being remotely amused gone, 'I can be an even bigger bastard than you think I am, Miss Harding,' he threatened, 'so don't push your luck.' With that he opened the door, and they entered his apartment.

It was a roomy, spacious apartment, Joss saw, well furnished to the point of quiet luxury. It was a masculine apartment, though, with no sign of flowers or a woman's touch. She had an intuitive feeling that were Thane Addison to have a wife he would in all probability want her to travel with him wherever he went, and it was quite unthinkingly that she queried, 'You're not married?'— and wished she had spared her breath.

'Rest easy!' he rapped, once again the snarling brute she was getting to know. 'I never *ever*,' he stressed, 'mix business with *that* sort of pleasure!'

Several hot retorts rushed to Joss's lips. But, just in time, she bit them back. She was tired, and if he had driven from Alexandria to Cairo and back again within the last eight hours, then he must be tired too. But as she received the message that, while there was some space in his life for women—and the virile look of him backed that up—she had no need to lock her bedroom door that night, that thought triggered off another.

'Do I have a bedroom to go to?' she asked him coolly, since he had dispensed with the word 'please,' not seeing why she should resurrect it.

'I'd better show you over the place,' he said brusquely, and she received yet another message—that he didn't want her blundering into his room in the middle of the night looking for the bathroom.

Perhaps I'm being over-sensitive, she thought a moment later as he began to show her where the kitchen and other rooms lay. It was a well-fitted kitchen, and in keeping with the rest of the apartment, but she guessed, since he would be moving on once this job was done, that the flat most likely was company-owned and did not specifically belong to him, but was there for the sole use of Beacon's Oil's highest.

'Are you hungry?' it occurred to him to query once they'd done the rounds of the flat.

Joss shook her head. 'I just want my bed—I've been up since...' Her voice faded at his curt look, and, convinced that he was about to bite something to the effect of 'save me from complaining women,' she clamped her lips together and went over and picked up her suitcase.

'Are you too tired to make up your own bed?' he sarcastically wanted to know, when having collected linen and a blanket he took her to one of the spare bedrooms.

'Goodnight,' Joss replied frostily, fuming again when a moment later the firm closing of the door told her she had the room to herself.

The swine of a man! she raged as she opened out the sheets he had given her. My heavens, what an uncivilised brute! she seethed, as she shook a pillow into a pillowcase.

Having made her bed, she visited the bathroom across the hall, washed her face and cleaned her teeth with the bottled water provided and was heartily glad that she hadn't again met her 'host'. She had seen enough of him that day to last her a lifetime!

She undressed and got into bed, and relived everything that had taken place since she had met him—and in no time she was fuming again.

He'd actually warned her off! *He had actually warned her off!* Starting to become more enraged than ever, Joss fought to stay calm lest she go and seek Thane Addison out to tell him there and then exactly what he could do with his job.

Having attained a modicum of calm some five minutes later, she remembered how, on the way here from Cairo, she had determined that she was good at her job and that she would jolly well show him. How the dickens, though, could she show him how good she was, if at the first hurdle she went running back to England?

She would stay, she wouldn't run, no matter how insulting Thane Addison was, she decided—though she couldn't think that he could improve on the insult he had already served her. She wasn't ready to go back anyway, she thought as sleep claimed her—not until she'd seen those Pyramids, anyhow!

CHAPTER THREE

HAVING slept soundly once she had got off to sleep, Joss awakened on Tuesday and, remembering that she was not in England but in Egypt, she smiled. Then she remembered *him* and her smile swiftly faded.

That he had actually had the unmitigated nerve to threaten dismissal—for that seemed to be his idea of disciplining someone—should she so far forget what a thoroughly detestable brute he was and fall in love with him, still irked her.

But she was there to work, not to lie in bed imagining pleasant fates that might befall him, such as falling down the stairs and breaking a leg or something of an equally charming nature—she wouldn't even offer him a temporary splint!

That for someone she hated Thane Addison was occupying so much space in her head seemed only natural to Joss as she pushed back the covers and reached for her robe. She couldn't hear him moving around, but she had a feeling that he was the type of man who survived on very little sleep.

She was proved right about that, in as much as that as she left her room and made for the bathroom, she discovered that he was already up and about—and showered too, she observed. For just as she went to open the bathroom door so he, robe- and nothing else-clad as far as she could make out from the bare hair-roughened chest and bare straight legs to be seen, came out. His fair hair was still wet and a few shades darker, she saw, and then noticed that as she was taking him in, he was taking in her robe-clad, tousle-haired self.

'Good morning,' she mumbled.

'Use the bottled water to clean your teeth,' he grunted, then they passed each other—she to go into the bathroom and he to go striding to his bedroom.

As Joss stretched out a hand to turn on the shower she saw that her hand was shaking from the encounter. Most odd, she deliberated, but then she was unused to hating anybody.

Back in her room, she quickly dressed in a lightweight business-looking two-piece and quickly applied the small amount of make-up that she wore. Then, knowing without a shadow of a doubt that wherever she slept that coming night it most definitely wouldn't be in this apartment, she quickly stripped the bed and folded the bedding. All that remained was to fasten her case and then go and find out what happened now.

Leaving her case for the moment, she took up her shoulder-bag and went looking for Thane Addison. She found him sitting in the kitchen. He was immaculately suited, wore a white shirt and silk tie and, she realised, was quite good-looking. He was already at work, she saw, and was scanning some typewritten notes which he held in one hand, while in his other hand he held a cup of coffee.

'There's coffee in the pot,' he looked up to inform her, seemed to approve of what she was wearing, then frowned and had gone back to the typed pages he held when he instructed, 'Make yourself toast.'

Because she was both thirsty and hungry Joss found the bread and popped a piece in the toaster and poured herself a cup of coffee. Silence reigned in the kitchen as she tracked down butter and marmalade.

Soundlessly she ate her repast. Without saying a word that might interrupt his concentration, she downed her coffee. He, she saw from the plate on the draining-board, must have finished his toast before she'd got to the kitchen.

He'd emptied his coffee-cup too, she noted, and, rather than just sit looking at him once she too had finished, she gathered up all the used dishes and washed and dried them. When she turned round, though, and took a glance in his direction, it was to see that he had ceased studying the papers in his hand, and was watching her!

'It's just that I've a tidy mind,' she told him shortly, not wanting him to think she was taking advantage of the domestic scene to get through any barrier he might put up.

'I'm glad to hear it!' he retorted grittily, and, taking up his briefcase from the floor beside him, he inserted his papers, snapped it to, then demanded, 'Ready?'

Joss knew from his tone that it was more than her life was worth to tell him no. And she went swiftly after him as, seeming now to be in something of a hurry, he went striding to the outer door.

At the door, however, he stopped so abruptly that she almost cannoned into him—only by a hair's breadth did she avoid a collision. Which, she would have thought, since this was clearly 'I hate female secretaries week', would have pleased him.

But not so. For, giving her a superior look from his much taller height, 'It was never my intention,' he drawled, 'to have you as my permanent guest.'

'What?' she queried, wondering what that had got to do with the fact that she had only just managed to keep from wrapping herself around him.

'Your case, Miss Harding,' he enlightened her stonily, 'your case!'

Pink colour stained her face as Joss remembered her suitcase in one of his spare bedrooms. Without a word she went to collect it, and knew then that she was going to have to develop a very thick skin if she was going to work for him for any length of time.

'Thank God it's only for a month,' she muttered when she got back to him, and again, didn't care a damn whether he heard or whether he didn't. Though, as she glanced at his still granite expression as they left his apartment, she knew that there was no amusing him this morning.

Without comment he took her case from her and in long, easy strides made short work—with not a broken leg in sight—of the stairs. Not deigning to run to keep up with him, Joss went at her own smart pace. Her suitcase was in the boot and he was just getting into his car when she reached the passenger's door.

It crossed her mind, as they started off, to query where they were going. But she was feeling just then that she would tear her tongue out before she would ask him anything. To her way of thinking, he could be taking her anywhere. Yesterday she had thought she would be working in Cairo, but today here she was in Alexandria. Would they be journeying for another three hours before she got anywhere close to a typewriter?

Leaving her fate in the lap of the gods, Joss brought her thoughts away from her temporary and cantankerous boss and where she might or might not end up that day, and took pleasure from watching the busy scene they were passing through.

The traffic in Alexandria was as horrendous as Cairo, she thought. They went in for horn-blowing just the same, at any rate. It was interesting to see the way Western dress merged quite happily with Middle Eastern dress; though. In the main it seemed that most men were dressed in Western style, with only the occasional man dressed in the shoulder-to-ground-length galabiyah. Joss saw several women shrouded all in black, and many more with their hair completely covered so that only their faces were to be seen. The sun was shining, and she felt it to be quite warm when, to her wonderment, she saw one man done up to the neck in muffler and overcoat!

She was in the middle of thinking how the man would never survive an English winter if he thought this was cold when all at once she became aware that Thane Addison had slowed down and seemed to be looking for a parking spot.

Naturally, being him, he found one without difficulty. When he left the car, so did she. Although her fury at his sarcasm over her case had simmered down somewhat, though, she was still feeling cross enough not to want to talk to him as she kept pace with him.

When he halted, she halted, then followed him into a set of offices that seemed much the same as the offices she had been in in Cairo yesterday. This, she quickly realised, was Beacon House, Alexandria. To her surprise, for she was past expecting anything normal of Mr Thane Addison, he introduced her round.

'This is Halima, who efficiently deals with the switchboard and any callers,' he introduced the pretty Egyptian receptionist. 'Miss Harding will be with us for...' he broke off and flicked his glance to Joss, then continued '...only a month, I think you said?'

'That's right.' Joss smiled at Halima as she extended her hand, and stayed cool in the knowledge that he had not missed her muttered 'Thank God it's only for a month' back at his flat.

Thane Addison then introduced a man who appeared out of nowhere at the sound of their voices, and who turned out to be Sami, the firm's Egyptian driver and general messenger. Then Thane was taking her into one of the other offices, and there she met a man of about thirty who was there to liaise with local Egyptian companies and who went by the name of Chad Woollams. 'Josslyn Harding,' Thane completed the introduction.

'Joss,' she shortened her name as Chad Woollams took her hand, and she cared not a light that her temporary boss was giving her a sharp look. In point of fact she was quite glad of any chance to show him that, while she was quite happy to let anyone use the more friendly shortened version of her name, she intended to be Josslyn, or preferably Miss Harding, to him for the duration of her stay.

'They never had anyone who looked half as good as you working at Beacon House, London, while I was there,' Chad Woollams offered with a warm smile.

'If you'll let Miss Harding have her hand back, Woollams, we can get on,' Thane Addison cut in sharply.

As if scalded, Chad Woollams let go of her hand. 'I'll see you,' he said bravely as Thane Addison took hold of her elbow and propelled her out—and into the next office.

The office next door housed Beacon Oil's Arabic-speaking, Egypt-stationed legal representative. Richard Maybury was a stocky man of about forty-four, who had a degree in English law, and a sound grounding of Egyptian law. He and Thane Addison, Joss learned, were working closely together on the contract which Thane had been brought in to sort out.

'Glad to know you, Josslyn,' Richard smiled as they shook hands.

Joss thought that to invite him too to use the shortened version of her name in front of Thane Addison might be overdoing it, so she stayed quiet, and, after a few minutes spent with the other man in business discussion, Thane took her to where she would work.

Her office was on the first floor, and was pleasant enough, being light and airy, and with an up-to-the-minute typewriter, similar to the one she used in London.

'My office is through this door here,' Thane told her, and went through to return a moment later with a handful of dictaphone tapes. 'A present for you,' he said, placing them down on her desk, and, with a look in his eye which she translated as saying 'that little lot should keep you quiet for a while', he told her, 'I have to go out,' and left her to it.

Joss was glad to see him go. At a guess, she thought, since Paula Ingram had been so unceremoniously sent packing, she probably had the whole of a week's work to get on with. Which was fine by her—at last she was about to start work.

An hour later she was deeply immersed in her task and discovering, somewhat to her surprise, that Thane Addison's voice on tape was quite pleasant—and that she rather liked the sound of it.

Clot, she derided; it wasn't that she liked his voice so well, but that she liked his way of working. For she could not fault anything about his crisp, clear sentences, and indeed found that she was most impressed that he could dictate great long tracts—a lot of it highly technical—with not an 'um' or an 'er' in sight.

Soon she was deeply immersed in her work again and had no idea that another hour had gone by until the door opened and Halima came in with a cup of coffee.

'I thought you might be ready for a cup of coffee, Miss Harding,' the pretty young Egyptian woman smiled.

Joss thanked her, and invited, 'Call me Joss,' and they spent a few minutes in friendly conversation, with Joss, who needed some Egyptian currency, discovering that there was a bank nearby.

'It will close at twelve-thirty,' Halima was just telling her when a buzzer she had switched on before leaving the switchboard sounded. 'I have a call!' she exclaimed, and swiftly disappeared.

Feeling she had earned a short break, Joss went to the bank, to return to her desk feeling much better for having more currency than the small amount she had been allowed to bring into the country.

She still had a lot of work to get through, however, and not having seen Thane Addison since his parting 'I have to go out' comment, she was soon pounding her typewriter again.

She was halfway through what she realised was a highly confidential document when the door opened, and was left open, as Chad Woollams came in.

'Lunchtime!' he told her as he came a little closer.

'Already!' Joss exclaimed, and, taking a disbelieving look at her watch, she saw that it was a quarter to one. 'Good heavens—the morning's flown!' she told him, feeling faintly staggered that a minute ago it had been eleven-fifteen.

'Then one can only suppose you're enjoying your work,' Chad remarked with a smile, and as Joss realised with a feeling of shock that she had enjoyed the work she'd done that morning and found it far more inter-esting and stimulating than the work she did for Mr Edwards back in England, Chad went on, 'I've come to take you to lunch.'

'Lunch?' she replied blankly, her thoughts still deep in the document she had been typing.

'You will lunch with me, won't you, Joss?' he smiled winningly.

Joss thought perhaps she would. But she never got to tell him so, because just then the man who she had evidence had the sharpest ears was suddenly standing in the open doorway, and it was he who answered for her.

'Miss Harding already has a lunchtime appointment, Woollams,' he told him curtly.

'Oh!' Chad spun round, startled. 'Er—I'll see you later, then, Joss,' he turned back to smile, but when Thane Addison stepped into the room and left the doorway free, he quickly left her office.

Joss didn't argue. Perfect secretaries—and that was what she was going to show him she was—knew better. She had not forgotten his 'You're sure about that?' comment when she had told him that she'd been given the Egypt job on merit and not via the 'old pals' network.

So, she asked, 'Have I got time to finish this page?'

'Depends how fast you type,' he answered curtly, and as Joss slammed into her typewriter, he came and picked up the work she had typed that morning.

Somehow she found his presence unnerving, but she typed through to the end of the page and, having managed to hold on to her nerve and complete her typing without the smallest error, she set the page down on the desk. Then, knowing she had no time to type anything else, she tidied up her desk.

She knew there was some comment about to break from Thane Addison as he handed her the typed pages he had been studying, though she very much doubted that she would be on the receiving end of any praise from him.

Nor was she, but she had to admit to a tiny feeling of agreeable surprise when he drawled, 'Well, well, a secretary who can spell "kinematic viscosity"!'

'You should see how I handle the really difficult ones!' Joss murmured coolly, and when the feeling of wanting to smile almost fractured her cool front, she bent her head and collected up the tapes he had given her. 'Do we have a safe?' she asked a moment later when she had control of her never-before-known peculiar sense of humour.

'There's one in my office, and Richard Maybury has one,' Thane Addison replied, and signed for her to follow him.

His office, Joss saw, was large, as was his desk and, as she had that morning realised, his work load. Which therefore made it a little surprising that his desk-top was absolutely clear. His briefcase seemed to go most places with him, she realised, suddenly spotting that he held it in his left hand. He had, though, put his briefcase in the safe and had turned to take the tapes and her morning's typing from her when it occurred to her that he must carry a lot of his work in his head too.

The tapes and the typing were locked in his safe when, from his lofty height, he turned to look down at her, and that was when Joss's curiosity got out of hand. Despite her stubborn intention not to ask him what the lunchtime appointment was that prevented her from accepting Chad Woollams' invitation, she could not keep it back any longer.

'Will I need to bring anything?' she questioned, and found that Thane Addison had no trouble in following her train of thought.

'We're having a business lunch, but you can leave your notepad behind.'

They were in his car and driving through the hurly-burly of Alexandria's traffic when Joss asked him, 'Can you tell me what my role is during this business lunch?'

'Your *role*, Miss Harding, is that of my secretary,' he replied aloofly.

'I—see,' she said as levelly as she could, when in actual fact she suddenly felt again like boxing his ears—how this man had the most uncanny knack of rubbing her up the wrong way! She rather thought he did it on purpose—she knew she was his secretary, for goodness' sake! Refraining from thanking God again that the job was only temporary, she took a controlling breath. 'Perhaps, Mr Addison,' she went on, knowing for certain that they must be lunching with one other person at least—for anything he wanted to discuss solely with her about business could be done in the office, without his needing to take her out to lunch, 'perhaps there might be one or two matters which you might care to brief me about. Who, for instance...'

'Your brief, Miss Harding,' he clipped, 'will be to keep your eyes and ears open.'

Now we're getting somewhere, she thought. 'We're meeting someone from a British firm?' she queried, feeling, since he knew she couldn't speak Arabic, that she must be being instructed to listen carefully to what their English-speaking business person had to say.

'My lunch guest is Mr Yazid Rashwan,' he soon, confusingly, scuttled the logic of her thinking.

'Oh!' she exclaimed, and then, having not only heard Yazid Rashwan's name before, but having come across it several times in her work that morning, she was pleased to be able to identify him. 'Mr Rashwan works for the Osiris Corporation, doesn't he?' she questioned.

'Yazid Rashwan,' Thane Addison informed her, '*is* the Osiris Corporation!'

Joss opened her mouth, then fell silent. The Osiris Corporation was the company Beacon Oil were keen to sign a contract with, and she was lunching with the man who *was* the Osiris Corporation—whew!

The rest of the journey did not take long, and then her boss, who it seemed had told her all he thought she should know, was drawing up outside a large hotel which was lapped by the waters of the Mediterranean.

It was then, as Thane escorted her into the hotel, that she began to feel quite unexpectedly proud to be walking alongside the tall, good-looking troubleshooter-in-chief of Beacon Oil.

Because her boss was playing host to Mr Rashwan, they had arrived courteously ahead of him, and as they waited for him to arrive Joss started to feel very thrilled, too, that she had been included in this meeting.

What sort of business was to be discussed, though, she was interested to see. For, having witnessed herself that Thane Addison had deliberately left his briefcase back at the office, she began to conclude that—for all it was very much the wish of Beacon Oil to have a contract signed—it seemed that any business to be discussed would be done so very informally.

Yazid Rashwan, when he arrived, was a slightly portly man of about fifty. He was as smartly and as immaculately tailored as her boss, Joss saw. So too was the man who was about half Mr Rashwan's age, and who accompanied him.

'My friend!' Yazid Rashwan greeted Thane Addison warmly, and in perfect English. 'We have kept you waiting?'

'Not at all, Yazid,' Thane replied as the two shook hands.

'You know my son, Khalil,' Yazid included the young man with him. 'You do not mind that he joins us?'

'Of course not,' Thane replied smoothly, as he shook hands with Khalil Rashwan, then turned to introduce the slender woman by his side. 'Josslyn arrived from England yesterday to help me with my paperwork,'

Thane went on easily, and, quite peculiarly, Joss felt her heart skip a ridiculous beat to hear, from the sound of it, that he intended to use her first name.

'Miss Ingram is no longer here?' Yazid queried.

'She had to return to England rather urgently on a matter unconnected with her work,' Thane told him easily.

'Am I not to be introduced to Josslyn?' Khalil Rashwan suddenly butted in, his eyes making a meal of Joss's face and ash-blonde hair.

'Do not be impatient, my son,' his father smiled, but his son was impatient, it seemed, for, not waiting for anyone to introduce him, he took hold of her right hand.

'I am Khalil Rashwan,' he told her, and as he shook hands with her, in the same perfect English as his parent, 'My father sends me to other countries very frequently to further my knowledge of the oil industry, but I am pleased that I am in Egypt at this time.'

Joss was a little nonplussed to know quite how to deal with this man who was still holding her right hand. But her cool unflappable manner stood her in good stead as, retrieving her hand, she replied non-committally, 'Your work must be very interesting.'

'Shall we find the dining-room?' Thane Addison suggested, and as his glance skimmed over her without lighting particularly on her, Joss knew she had somehow earned herself another black mark.

Because he was an admirable host, however, the mealtime passed without anyone but her being aware that she had somewhere, it seemed, put a foot wrong. She decided to put it to the back of her mind and concentrate on the business in hand. Though, although both Osiris and Beacon were mentioned, as far as she could tell, nothing of a very specific nature to do with the contract—which was what this business lunch was all about—was discussed.

Not, she had to admit, that she caught everything that was being said, because Khalil Rashwan, who had seated himself next to her, seemed to have no interest in business and would often make some comment to her while the other two men were in easy conversation.

'Did I hear that you arrived only yesterday?' he questioned as the four of them sat drinking an after-lunch coffee.

'Yes. I . . .'

'But you can have seen nothing of Alexandria yet?' he butted in, and promptly declared, his warm gaze fixed intently on her brown eyes and creamy skin, 'I will attend to that straight away!'

Joss strove hard not to blink at the young man's open enthusiasm. He might well have been a couple of years older than she, but he seemed to her to be a couple of years younger. She was conscious, however, that she must do nothing that might offend him, though she was unsure if Thane Addison—from a business point of view—would approve or disapprove if she accepted what she thought was an invitation from Khalil—who had already told her that she must use his first name.

'Actually, Khalil,' she told him lightly after some moments, 'I'm here to work.'

'But you cannot work all the time!' he exclaimed at once, and decided on the spot, 'I will show you some of Alexandria this afternoon.' He broke off, paused only briefly, then went on enthusiastically, 'This afternoon I will take you to the Greco-Roman Museum.'

Starting to feel uncomfortably that she stood a grave risk of offending Khalil, Joss glanced at Thane. Had she hoped that he might step in and help her out, however, she would have been sorely disappointed. Though she had prior warning that she was wasting her time in looking to him for direction, when she caught the cool way he met her glance.

She could, none the less, have done without what she considered his sarcastic, snide remark, as he told her evenly, 'You mustn't neglect your education, Josslyn.'

'There!' Khalil straight away seized on what he saw as her boss's permission. 'We have finished lunch. We will go now and...'

'I'm sorry, Khalil,' Joss interrupted him quickly, speaking instinctively and not giving herself time to think, 'but I have a great deal of work waiting for me at my desk. It's impossible for me to go with you today. Thank...'

'Tomorrow, then,' he interrupted her quickly, and while she was getting over the way he was insisting on being her guide at some stage, he was getting to his feet. 'I'm sure that my father and Thane have matters to discuss which do not concern us—shall we take a walk outside?'

As Joss saw it, there was little she could do but agree. For all she knew, Khalil Rashwan might have been told to accompany his father for the precise reason of getting Thane's secretary out of the way so that the two men could have an off-the-record business discussion which might benefit both companies. Yazid Rashwan was smiling approvingly anyway, she observed, and although a quick glance at her boss showed that Thane was not smiling, neither was he commanding her to stay exactly where she was.

'That would be pleasant,' she told Khalil lightly, and excusing herself to the two men, she left the table and went with Khalil from the hotel, which stood in isolation but with the grounds and attractive pink and white minareted building of the Montazah Palace standing very near by.

Joss had been wondering what she should talk to Khalil about, but she need not have worried, for he did all the talking necessary, though it was true, most of his talk took the shape of questions. Even though his questions were mainly about her life in England.

'So you have no special man friend in England?' he recapped as they strolled in the hotel grounds.

'I more often go out with a group of friends,' she replied, and got him off the subject when she noticed a car parked at the hotel that had been decorated with ribbons and bouquets of flowers. 'Is that a wedding car?' she asked him.

'Yes,' he replied, but did not have the interest she had in the romantic sight of flowers decorating the bumper, bonnet, boot and roof, while pom-poms of white ribbons adorned door-handles and wheel-hubs.

They were making their way back to the entrance when Thane Addison and Yazid Rashwan suddenly appeared. Joss made it to Thane's side just as he was shaking hands with Yazid. She made her own goodbyes and, feeling rather relieved that she had come from the business lunch without having committed herself to go to the Greco-Roman Museum with Khalil Rashwan tomorrow, she went quickly—to keep up with Thane's stride—to his car.

She was in the passenger seat and Thane was driving away from the hotel when she wondered if he had actually conducted any business with Yazid Rashwan. She considered the matter for a moment or two, then decided that as Thane Addison's secretary—albeit temporarily—she should naturally show an interest.

'Were you able to bring negotiations any nearer to a satisfactory conclusion?' she opened her mouth to make the interested business enquiry—and wished she'd kept her mouth closed.

'You're that concerned?' he snarled back at her for her trouble.

'What's that supposed to mean?' she enquired, heated in a second.

'From where I was sitting, you were more concerned in encouraging the overtures of Yazid Rashwan's son!' he barked toughly.

'I was not!' Joss protested vehemently. 'All I did was try to be polite. To...'

'He couldn't take his eyes off you!'

'I didn't do anything to...'

'You don't have to do anything,' Thane Addison abruptly cut in again. 'It's the way you look!'

'I can't help the way I look!' she snapped, and was ignored for her trouble.

Swine! she fumed, and glared at him. She looked away when, his jaw jutting aggressively, he showed himself impervious to her ire. They were nearly back at the office when it occurred to her to wonder if there might not have been some sort of back-handed compliment in his comment, 'It's the way you look.' She shrugged the thought aside. As if she cared! The man was a monster.

'Hello, Halima!' she greeted the receptionist cheerfully when with Thane Addison striding in front of her she crossed the reception floor.

'Hello, Joss,' the other girl smiled, and Joss went up to her own office and cared not that her boss had gone in the direction of Richard Maybury's office.

That was to say that as far as she was concerned he could go to hell and the sooner the better—but not before he had unlocked his safe and given her back the work she had been in the middle of.

Expecting that he would come up to his office at any moment, Joss fumed about him for a while. Wretched man, she thought irately, then remembered that he still had her case in the back of his car and that she had no idea of where she would be camping out that night. Not that she'd ask him—she'd be damned if she would!

Fifteen minutes went by, and when she realised that in all that time, and with loads of work to be done, she had done nothing but twiddle her thumbs, she was of the opinion that this was ridiculous.

In the next moment she had the phone in her hand and was asking Halima if Mr Addison had gone out.

'He's in conference with Mr Maybury, I think,' Halima answered, and before Joss could tell her not to, 'I'll put you through,' she said, and efficiently did so.

'Joss Harding here,' Joss said when Richard Maybury answered his phone. 'Is Mr Addison with you?'

'Just a minute,' he replied, and the next she knew was that her taciturn boss was on the line.

'Addison,' he announced.

'Josslyn Harding,' she replied, keeping her tones as level and as courteous as she could. 'May I have my work from the safe, please?' she requested, and hated him some more when without another word he put the phone down on her.

Ignorant pig! she railed, and got up and went to look unseeing out of the window. She was still there when she heard his footsteps on the stairs. She heard him go into his office by another door, and saw no reason to move until the door connecting their two offices opened and he came through with the work she had given him to lock away before lunch.

'Thank you,' she said politely, and found her politeness wasted when, without comment, he strode out.

That man! she thought, enraged, and took her fury out on her typewriter. Fortunately she was an accurate typist, so that even in her temper she achieved quite a lot of error-free work that afternoon.

She had a break for a cup of tea at about four o'clock, but, knowing that she had a lot of last week's work to catch up on, was soon busy at her typewriter again. She hardly thought it was out of consideration for her and the backlog she had to cope with that Thane Addison had not given her any dictation that day. He'd probably give her a double helping tomorrow, she realised—if in fact he wasn't somewhere right at this moment dictating another load on to tape.

When a moment's weariness took her and she paused to stretch her back, the thought again occurred—where would she be sleeping that night? She started to type again, and was still of the view that she was not going to ask, when it suddenly struck her that, stuck away up here the way she was, being a new member of staff, she could easily be forgotten! For all she knew, Thane Addison could have finished discussing legal matters with Richard Maybury, and could have left the building hours ago!

Joss was on the point of being certain that everyone would leave Beacon House that evening without giving her another thought, and that she would be spending the night locked in where she was, when suddenly the door opened.

Without so much as a grunt Thane Addison came over and took a look at the vast amount of typing she had got through. Then, 'You've done enough for today,' he told her. 'Clear your desk.'

Striving hard to hold down some sarcastic comment to the effect that he should watch it, that he had almost given her praise, Joss began to tidy her desk. Since there

were only seven minutes to go before five o'clock, she
didn't thank him either for his intimation that she could
pack up for the day. Though on reflection she realised
that he would probably, either here or at his apartment,
be working on into the evening. She doubted anyway
that his working day stopped at five.

Having handed to him anything that had to be housed
in the safe that night, she was busying herself putting
the cover on her typewriter when he came back into her
office.

'Ready?' he questioned.

For answer, Joss picked up her shoulder-bag. She had
no idea where they were going, but unless he was taking
her to some meeting or other—and his 'You've done
enough for today' remark rather precluded that—she
guessed he was taking her to her new abode.

She was still of the view that wild horses would not
make her ask him, and, having taken her lead from his
taciturn manner, she determined that unless she had
something very necessary to say, she would say nothing.

Having expected that she would be staying in some
quite decent but moderately priced accommodation, the
amazement she experienced when he stopped the car
outside a newish and luxurious-looking hotel loosened
her tongue. When he got out and began to extract her
case from the boot, she too got out of the car.

'I'm staying here?' she asked in astonishment.

'We can't have Khalil Rashwan thinking we're paupers
when he comes calling,' he drawled, nastily, she thought.

Tilting her chin an angry fraction higher, Joss clamped
her lips shut and went with him into the hotel. Apparently she was expected, so she guessed then that, had
she thought to ask Halima if she had any idea where she
would be staying, there was a good chance that Halima

would have been able to tell her that Thane Addison had contacted this hotel at some time during that day.

Thane Addison waited only to see that she was checked in without any hitch—and she refused to be grateful to him for that—then he was telling her, 'Sami will be on hand to collect you in the morning and to bring you back in the evening.' Then he was gone.

Her room was excellent, but any pleasure she might have found at being so housed faded as she recalled Thane's sarcastic comment, 'We can't have Khalil Rashwan thinking we're paupers.'

Deciding to put Mr Thane Addison and his acid tongue from her mind, Joss set about unpacking and, since Beacon Oil very definitely weren't paupers, she decided a little room service wouldn't break them. She phoned down and ordered a pot of tea.

The tea had arrived and she was in the middle of writing an 'everything's marvellous' letter to her parents, who would worry themselves silly at any hint that her life was not a bed of roses, when the phone suddenly rang.

Expecting it to be a wrong number, Joss went to answer it, and got the shock of her life to hear Khalil Rashwan on the other end. She was still in the throes of wondering how on earth he had managed to find out which hotel she was in, when she realised that he was asking her out to dinner.

'Oh, I'm sorry, Khalil,' she told him pleasantly, 'but I've not long checked in here, and I've one or two things I must do.'

'We can dine in the hotel, if you're tired,' he pressed eagerly.

'Actually, I'm not awfully hungry,' she told him, quite liking the man, but not sure that she cared to be pursued so assiduously. 'I ate a big meal at lunchtime,' she reminded him.

'Very well,' he agreed at last, then went on to state, 'I shall look forward to showing you the Museum tomorrow as we agreed. Shall I call for you at your office?'

Just at that moment Joss could not in truth remember if she had agreed to go to the Museum with him the next day, or if she hadn't. But, since his father *was* the Osiris Corporation, and since she didn't know that Khalil might report back to his father that someone from Beacon Oil had broken their word to him, she could see nothing else for it.

'That would be nice,' she replied, not really seeing how a secretary's breaking an agreement could in any way affect the agreement Thane was trying to reach, but not wanting to be the one to put the smallest spanner in the works. 'Is one o'clock all right?' she asked Khalil, and put the phone down a few minutes later knowing herself committed, and hoping against hope that the Museum could be 'done' in an hour—her lunch hour.

She had only just picked up the pen she had put down and had written no more than half a line when to her surprise her phone rang again. Warily, hoping that it was not Khalil ringing again for some reason, she went and picked the phone up—then got another shock.

'Who were you talking to just now?' Thane Addison demanded. And when, stunned, she was wondering how on earth he knew she had been speaking to anyone, he went on shortly—she not being swift enough in her replies, apparently—'Khalil Rashwan rang wanting your address. Are you dining with him?' he demanded to know.

For all of two seconds Joss was ready to let Thane Addison run for an answer. But that was before she realised that, with the negotiations he was conducting proving so troublesome, maybe he had a right to keep his finger on every pulse.

So, thinking that, in view of his remarks about her encouraging Khalil at lunchtime, it would please him, she began, 'No, I refused...'

Abruptly, she was interrupted, and Thane was sounding not pleased at all when, 'You haven't offended him?' he rapped.

'Of course I haven't!' she flared, angry that he thought she couldn't handle things better than that. 'I'm seeing him tomorrow...' she went to go on to illustrate how Khalil couldn't have been offended. But the line was suddenly dead. Thane Addison had crashed his phone down.

'Swine!' muttered Joss as she snapped her phone back on its rest. From where *she* was sitting, it seemed she couldn't do anything right—no matter which way she jumped!

CHAPTER FOUR

Joss breakfasted on croissants, jam and coffee the next morning, then returned to her room to check her appearance. She wondered fleetingly if she should take with her the leather zip-up document wallet which she had packed at the last minute, and decided it would do no harm. She might never need to use it, but it would take up little space if she left it in the office—that way she would be ready for any eventuality.

At half-past eight she left her room and took the lift to the ground floor. Thane Addison had told her that Sami would collect her, but naturally it would never have occurred to His Grumpiness to tell her at what time.

Pleasingly, however, the first person she saw as she made her way to the automatic glass outer doors was Sami. 'Good morning!' he beamed happily, and as she smilingly replied to his cheerful greeting, 'Shall I carry your briefcase?' he enquired helpfully.

'I can manage,' she smiled, and as he escorted her to a smart-looking car and held the passenger door open for her, her smile extended deep within her. She was in Alexandria, and suddenly she was feeling very good about it.

The feeling was doomed not to last. For one thing, although they reached the office unscathed, Sami was not the cool driver that her boss was. Joss wryly considered that car horn manufacturers in the city must do a roaring replacement trade. She had heard of people driving on their brakes, but in Egypt, it seemed that everyone drove on their car horn.

Thanks to Sami's driving, however, she was at the office well before nine. 'Thank you, Sami,' she told him as, trying to look as though she had never tensed up once in the certainty of a collision, she got out of the car.

'I will be here for you at five o'clock,' he promised with a wide grin.

What could she do under the threat of such a treat? 'Thank you,' she murmured again, and pushed her way into Beacon House.

'Good morning, Joss,' Halima, as ever smiling, greeted her, and as Joss went over and exchanged a few pleasantries with her, the outer door opened and Chad Woollams came in.

'Say you'll have lunch with me today,' he addressed her without preamble.

'I've only just had breakfast!' she laughed.

'I know, but I've a feeling that I've got to get in early if I'm to have the privilege of your sole company.'

Chad's brash manner amused her. She had come across his type before, and knowing him to be completely harmless, she felt in no way uncomfortable. 'Sorry, Chad,' she smiled at him, 'you're not early enough— I've a previous appointment for lunchtime.'

She was on her way up the stairs when he recovered sufficiently to call after her, 'What about dinner tonight?'

'What about lunch tomorrow?' she called back.

'You're on!' he grinned, and she rather gathered that she had walked straight into that one.

She had the trace of a rueful smile on her face when she entered her office, but she straightened her expression at once the moment she saw through the open communicating door that Thane Addison was first in.

She remembered the bad-tempered way he had slammed the phone down on her the evening before, and was in two minds about giving him the courtesy of a greeting. Then he looked up from his work, and she suddenly found herself staring into his piercing grey eyes.

'Good morning,' she said coolly, and turned away to go to her desk.

She had stowed away her document wallet and her bag when she noticed that the work she had last night put away in the safe was now on her desk. Quite clearly she was meant to get on with it with all speed. She did.

The communicating door remained open, and when at eleven o'clock Halima brought in a tray containing two cups of coffee, Joss took a break. Halima took a cup of coffee in to Thane Addison and returned to Joss's office, but, unlike yesterday, she did not seem disposed to stay for a chat.

Joss sipped her coffee after Halima had gone and then, having collected several queries during her two hours of work, she took her business queries, and a personal one of her own, into the adjoining office.

'Is it convenient for me to see you with some queries?' she enquired, as finding a clear space on his desk she put down some completed confidential and faultless typing.

'What's your problem?' he asked and, encouragingly, sounded civil enough.

In no time at all he had dealt with every one of her business queries. But when Joss did not at once move away, he gave her a cool look of enquiry, and she sensed that he was impatient to get on.

'Something else worrying you?' he clipped uninvitingly.

'Not worrying, exactly,' she replied quickly, and guessing that his mood was not going to sweeten in any way for being kept hanging about, 'It's just that Khalil Rashwan is calling for me at one to take me to a museum, and I'm just not sure if I'll be able to make it back to the office for two o'clock.'

She saw Thane Addison's face darken, and knew that she was about to receive the sharp edge of his tongue at any minute. Surprisingly, though, he must have bitten back any acid remark. His, 'What do you expect me to do about it?' however, held acerbity in full measure.

'Nothing!' she replied in a heated moment—then gained control of a temper that this man had to do very little to unleash, and added in a dignified way, 'That is, I was wondering if I might have an extended lunch hour? Naturally,' she went on quickly, 'I shall work late tonight.'

For about five seconds he leaned back in his chair and grey eyes pierced steady, unflappable brown ones, then, 'Naturally you will,' he agreed. And, as she gathered from that that she had the extended lunch hour she had requested, he stretched out a hand to take up the completed work she had given him, and drawled, 'You're a fast worker, Miss Harding.'

Joss returned to her desk knowing full well that the man she at present had the misfortune to be working for had not been complimenting her on the speed of her output, but on the swiftness with which she had got herself a date with the son of a man who *was* the Osiris Corporation.

She again slammed into her typewriter and, the work she was then engaged upon being of a less tricky nature, she found that her thoughts were wandering. Looked at in that context, she supposed Khalil Rashwan could be termed as something of a catch. Not that she was interested in him that way. He was a pleasant enough man, but in her view, though older in years, not mature enough for her.

Why her thoughts should suddenly grasshopper on to Thane Addison suddenly, she had no idea. But all at once she discovered that she was thinking that Thane too could be termed as something of a catch! Grief! she thought in the next second—as if she was interested in *him*!

At half-past twelve she took some more work in to him, the last of anything of a confidential nature, and was certain that—for all his eligibility—she pitied any poor woman who was so soft in the head as to be interested in him.

'Have you plenty to get on with when you do make it back?' he had the nerve to ask when she was about to return to her office.

Swallowing down a snappy 'I'll make it last', Joss managed to stay calm. 'I think I'm about halfway through the backlog,' she said as evenly as she could.

'Shouldn't like you to get bored,' he drawled, then stood up, and was towering over her as he added, 'I'm going to lunch now—I may not be back before you.'

'Bon appétit!' she bade him, and as he cleared his desk, in a suddenly cross frame of mind she returned to her office.

She did not look up when she heard the door from his office into the corridor open and close—she hoped he never came back. Which, she realised some minutes later, made it most odd that she should then start to think about how she had previously received the message that there was some space in his life for women. For suddenly she was remembering that he had told her on Monday night, 'I never *ever* mix business with *that* sort of pleasure.' She tied that in with the fact that he had gone to lunch early and had indicated that he would be late back. Her brow wrinkled crossly as she found herself wondering—was he then having an extended business lunchtime or a pleasure-filled one? Would she in fact see him at all that afternoon?

When Joss made ready to leave her office at one, she was little short of astounded to realise that she had spent quite some time in speculating about Thane Addison in an out-of-work context.

As if she cared, for crying out loud! she scorned, and went down the stairs to find Khalil Rashwan was already in reception waiting. 'Josslyn!' he beamed, stepping over to her.

'Hello, Khalil,' she replied, and in a friendly way she extended her right hand.

That was a mistake, for again he held it longer than necessary. However, once she had retrieved her hand and they were outside Beacon House, he was attentively showing her into the passenger seat of his opulent car and was talking of taking her to lunch.

'I'm afraid I haven't time to lunch *and* visit the Greco-Roman Museum,' she told him, as firmly as she felt she could in the circumstance of not wishing to offend him.

'But you must eat!' he protested. 'And I have reserved a table...'

Wondering at what time she would get back to her office, Joss compromised for a snack lunch, and Khalil agreed—the only complication being that no one seemed in any hurry to do anything. Khalil, certainly, seemed to have all the time in the world, and the smart restaurant to which he took her seemed to be of the belief that their clients would rather linger over even a snack meal than rush at it. It was therefore nearly two when they left the restaurant.

Relieved to be in the car and on her way to the Museum, Joss discovered that her relief was a little premature. For, having thought when Khalil stopped the car that they had arrived at the Museum, she discovered that he had brought her to a little park.

'Where . . . ?' she began to question.

'I thought you might like to see Pompey's Pillar,' he smiled, and escorted her up a good many steps to the tall monument that looked to be somewhere in the region of about ninety feet high.

'Er—thank you,' said Joss, and because she felt that he was really putting himself out for her enjoyment, she delved into the far reaches of her mind to try and remember if she'd ever heard of Pompey or his Pillar. 'Pompey—Julius Caesar's rival?' she dragged out of some dark corner to query.

But Khalil, smiling as ever, was shaking his head. 'No,' he told her, and furthered her education by telling her that the high granite monument was erected much later than Pompey's time, in honour of the Emperor Diocletian. They spent about ten minutes in wandering round the little park, where a carpet of small and bright yellow flowers spread out and mingled with artefacts of other centuries.

When at the end of that time Khalil announced that they would now go to the Museum, Joss, who had been battling not to look at her watch, was much relieved again.

She forgot about time for a while once they had entered the Museum, however, finding that the relics from Alexandria's Greek and Roman past were most interesting. Slowly they wandered from section to section, taking in sarcophagi, statues, reliefs and paintings as they went.

They were in a section which housed a vast coin collection, however, when Joss glanced at her watch and saw with astonishment and some alarm that she had already extended her lunch hour by one and a half hours.

'It's half-past three!' she exclaimed to Khalil, unable to conceal a little of her agitation.

'The time worries you?' he asked, and looked as though it was of some concern to him that she must not be worried.

'I have my work to do,' she told him, and glanced about for the exit.

'Thane Addison is—um—a slavedriver?' Khalil queried as, realising that she was now desirous of returning to her office, he escorted her from the building.

'Oh, no,' she replied to his question, realising that, for all that their conversation had nothing to do with the contract which Thane was there to negotiate, she was still a representative of Beacon Oil—her first loyalty, therefore, since she wouldn't be here but for her job, being due to them.

They were in Khalil's car and he was driving her back to Beacon House when she began to wish he had not mentioned Thane Addison's name—for the brute of a man now refused to be ejected from her mind.

If he was a slavedriver, then he drove himself just as hard, she had to admit. Though she thought it was fair to say that she drove herself pretty hard without anybody's help—and she enjoyed being busy. In actual fact, though, save for giving her those tapes yesterday, Thane had left her pretty much alone while she caught up, which couldn't, she mused, be called slavedriving in anybody's book.

That was, she mused, until one remembered—when she had more than enough to do—his 'Have you plenty to get on with?' remark before lunch. In remembering that remark, however, Joss was soon remembering her thoughts about *his* extended lunch hour.

Khalil was pulling his car up near Beacon House when Joss began to think that, depending on how Thane's 'lunchtime' had gone, she might not see him again that afternoon. And suddenly, and most strangely, she discovered that she did not know how she felt about that.

How very peculiar, she thought a moment later, and as Khalil walked with her to the door of Beacon House she shrugged away as ridiculous any absurd notion that she should feel anything at all where *that* man was concerned.

'May I dine with you tonight?' Khalil asked as she thanked him for lunch and for showing her a little of Alexandria's antiquities.

Joss thought briefly of how Beacon Oil commanded her loyalty, but then set that against the problems she might be storing up for herself later—she was here for a whole month, for goodness' sake!

'I'm sorry, Khalil,' she told him, half fearful that she might have Thane Addison breathe fire and brimstone if she offended Khalil and put the skids under the deal Thane was trying to do with his father. 'I've something else I must do tonight,' she added quickly—and felt enormously relieved when, although he looked a shade downcast, Khalil accepted her refusal without offence.

'I expect it is often this way for you,' he murmured sadly, then promised, 'I will telephone you.'

Joss said hello to Halima as she went in, and discovered that she felt sorely tempted to enquire if Mr Addison had returned from lunch. She pushed the question down, however, and decided that she hoped he had not returned, and that he would stay out for the rest of the day.

Which made it most irritating to her that her heart should hurry up a crazy beat when, going into her office, she saw through the open communicating door that Thane Addison was seated behind his large desk.

'I didn't expect to be this late—I'm sorry,' she braved the scowling look of him to enter his office and deliver the apology she felt was due.

'That makes two of us!' he grunted sarcastically, making her wish she'd let him run for his apology. 'Bring your shorthand pad in!' he ordered.

My stars! Joss thought when an hour later she reeled out of his office—and she'd denied that he was a slavedriver? She took herself back to her desk and hoped with all she had that she would be able to read back the masses of quick-fire dictation she had taken down in the last sixty minutes.

If she had worked strictly to the time she had taken out then she would have finished work around seven that evening. But her fingers were still flying over the typewriter keys at seven-thirty.

Thane Addison was working late too, but, finding the work she was doing for him totally absorbing, Joss was completely unaware of the time. She had just come to the end of a page and was in the act of removing it from her machine when she became conscious that he had left his desk and had come to stand in the doorway.

He appeared to be studying her to some degree, but, staying cool, she looked back at him. He filled the doorway, she noted, yet he had not an ounce of spare flesh. In fact, she saw, he was quite something of a man. Astonished at the way her thoughts were straying, for she could not remember taking so much detailed note of any man before, she hastily averted her eyes. At the same moment, he moved forward.

'You can leave the rest of that until the morning,' he told her.

Joss glanced at her watch, then flicked her glance at him. 'Is that the time?' she gasped.

'Why—going somewhere?' he challenged, his tone instantly aggressive, accusing almost.

'Not tonight!' Joss said hotly, instantly nettled, and indeed, she felt so annoyed that she cared not just then that he was her boss, as she added pointedly, 'Since I've been here I've discovered that there are occasions when I prefer my own company to anyone else's.'

She did not suppose she had offended him; in her view he had too thick a hide for anything she said to dent him. Though quite what she expected him to answer, she did not know. But she was glaring at him hostilely while he stared arrogantly back when, as if against his will, the corners of his mouth started to pick up.

Staring at him, she was as amazed as she had been once before when she had thought she had seen evidence that her tart tongue had amused him. But, as before, all sign of him being remotely amused was soon gone, and as he had done yesterday, he commanded, 'Clear your desk,' and returned to his office.

Five minutes later Joss had her desk cleared and, with the work she had placed in her desk drawers—it not being so confidential that it needed to be put in the safe—she had nothing to go into his office for.

Which therefore made her feel most awkward when she went slowly across her office carpet and waited while he secured his briefcase. Then he looked up. 'Er...' she said hesitantly, then took a grip on herself, 'Sami's gone for the day, I—er—suppose?' she made herself ask the question.

For a second Thane Addison looked back at her unspeaking. Then, 'You can find your own way to your hotel,' he told her arrogantly, 'or,' he added, and a mocking light had suddenly come to his eyes, 'take a lift in my company.'

Quickly, her lips twitching, Joss turned away. She had not expected it, but *he* had amused *her*. She hoped he hadn't noticed.

There was no chance of her lips twitching the next day. Thursday morning was busy to the point of being frantic, with Thane Addison, in Joss's opinion, being at his intolerant worst. To her mind, if he was out to disprove any outrageous rumour that he might have a sense of humour, then he couldn't have done a better job.

She was glad when it was lunchtime and she left her office to meet Chad Woollams in the reception area to go for a bite of lunch. But no sooner were they seated in a restaurant than she discovered that she was not the only one to feel the cutting edge of Thane Addison's tongue that morning.

'All I said was "Good morning" and he came down on me like a stack of coal,' Chad complained.

'For just saying "Good morning"?' Joss enquired.

'Well, I suppose he did have an axe to grind,' he admitted, honestly if reluctantly. 'He's laboured like stink to restart negotiations with Osiris when they got stuck in the mire. What he didn't need was for me to drag my feet and not contact Mr Ismail...'

'Mr Ismail?' queried Joss, the name somehow familiar as if she had typed it recently. 'Seif Ismail?' she remembered.

'The same,' Chad confirmed.

'Isn't he one of the Osiris Corporation's legal representatives?' she asked.

'They don't come much higher,' he told her. 'Unfortunately, I was up to my eyes in it yesterday when Mr Addison came back from a meeting and told me to fix up a meeting between Seif Ismail and Richard Maybury to discuss some legal snarl-up.'

'Oh dear,' murmured Joss, seeing for herself that Thane Addison, following up any morning greeting with a question of when had Chad arranged for the meeting of the two legal representatives to take place, would blow his top to be told that Chad had done nothing about it. Especially when Thane was working his socks off over this deal. 'You've—er—arranged the meeting now, I take it?'

'Are you kidding?' Chad laughed, starting to cheer up. 'Within two minutes of Mr Addison's chewing me up and spitting out the pieces I'd got Sami driving me over to Osiris to see Mr Ismail personally. He and Richard are meeting this afternoon. I guess you could say,' he opined after a few moments silence, 'that when Thane Addison wants something done—he gets results.'

'Will he get the agreement he wants with Osiris, do you think?' she asked.

'If *he* can't pull it off, then nobody can,' Chad replied, and spoke for some time of the many hurdles that had had to be overcome to get negotiations so far forward that the legal representatives of both companies, who had been working in an advisory capacity from the beginning, were now about to be brought into contact with each other. 'I can't see what other stumbling blocks will crop up,' he commented, 'but the whole thing's been fraught with one obstacle after another.'

Hence Mr Thane Addison, troubleshooter-in-chief, being called in, thought Joss as she and Chad left the restaurant and returned to Beacon House.

Thursday afternoon was no easier than the morning had been, and Joss returned to her hotel that evening hoping against hope that Khalil would not take it into his head to telephone. All she wanted to do was to put her feet up and recharge her batteries. She didn't think she had even sufficient energy to find a tactful way to tell him she didn't want to go out with him.

However, Khalil did not telephone her, and Joss went to bed to sleep soundly, and to start work on Friday and to have the day as hectic as the day before. Khalil did phone that night, but by then she had come up for air.

'I made myself not telephone you last evening, because I do not want you to get tired of me,' he told her with such charming honesty that Joss felt drawn to like him more than she had so far.

'Oh, Khalil,' she said softly, and was to regret that her tone must have been a shade warmer than she had meant it to be, because after that, it seemed that he was never off the phone.

She declined his invitation to go out with him on Friday night, and on Saturday accepted an invitation from Grace Maybury, Richard's wife, to go to their home for dinner. She was glad, therefore, that when Khalil phoned and asked her to dine with him on Saturday evening, she was able to truthfully plead a previous dinner engagement.

'Then you must dine with me tomorrow,' he insisted.

Joss thought about it for a moment, but couldn't really see any reason why she should not dine with him. He was a pleasant enough man. 'Could we dine in my hotel?' she asked, her mind on the gruelling day Monday might turn out to be, and how it might be an idea if she had an early night on Sunday.

'Anything you say!' he replied jubilantly, but he still rang her on Sunday to check that she had not forgotten.

Joss took to Grace Maybury when she dined with her and her husband on Saturday. And her dinner with Khalil went much better than she had anticipated. True, she would have preferred that he had not attempted to take possession of her left hand while she was trying to eat her rice, fish and jacket potato, but he'd soon got the message when she looked at him solemnly and quietly told him, 'I need that hand, Khalil.'

Sami was there to drive her to Beacon House on Monday morning, and Joss metaphorically squared her shoulders as she went into the building, to be ready to tackle anything Thane Addison might throw at her that week.

As seemed to be his habit, he was there before her and, for once, was quite civil as he bade her, 'Good morning.'

Someone's had a good weekend, she found herself thinking, quite sourly, she realised, so she brightly answered 'Good morning,' saw that his eyes were on the upward curve of mouth, and felt momentarily glad that some friend had once told her she had a beautiful mouth. Then she bent to stow away her shoulder-bag.

By the time she had done that, however, it was as if Thane Addison had decided he had been too civil, for, 'Come in here with your pad,' he was suddenly instructing coldly.

'One of these days he'll say "please" and I'll drop down dead,' Joss muttered as she went in. She took a seat and stared at him with sweet, innocent eyes when, going on past performances, she realised that he had probably picked up her mutterings on his never-miss-a-thing antennae.

He made no comment, however, but, as if he was bent on paying her back for her sauce, his dictation over the next forty minutes was, she would swear, more rapid than ever. Only just by the skin of her teeth managing to keep up with him, Joss couldn't have been more gratified when the phone in her office rang, and he broke off.

'Shall I go and answer it?' she enquired prettily, knowing full well that Halima would ring Thane's office for her if she didn't answer her own phone.

'Here!' he snarled, and, lifting his receiver, he pushed it at her.

'Hello, Halima—were you ringing me?' she asked when Halima came on the line.

'Mr Rashwan is calling you,' Halima replied, and as Joss realised that it would be Rashwan junior, not senior, Halima was putting him through.

'Josslyn?' he enquired.

'Yes. Hello, Khalil,' she answered, and saw Thane Addison make a short angry movement. Clearly he did not care to have his time wasted while she took personal calls.

'Josslyn, I am devastated,' Khalil began soulfully, and, while all she wanted to do was to terminate the call, he went on to tell her that since having met her he had forgotten he was scheduled to fly to Japan today. 'I thought it was next week,' he told her, and went on at some length about how, now of all times, it was entirely the wrong time to go.

It was entirely the wrong time for him to ring too, Joss saw as she flicked a glance at Thane and caught the icy blast of his angered gaze.

'Er—how long will you be away?' she asked Khalil when he paused for breath.

'A week—perhaps two,' he complained.

'Then I shall still be here when you get back,' she told him quickly, ready by then to say anything to get rid of him.

'You promise?' he questioned urgently.

Oh, help! Joss thought, and as Thane gave her a fierce look and seemed ready to snatch the phone out of her hand at any second, 'Yes, I promise,' she said recklessly.

Recklessly, because she was of the opinion just then that Thane Addison with his tendencies towards instant dismissal might be giving way to those tendencies at any moment. Shortly afterwards she told Khalil that she must go, and said goodbye to him.

'I trust you didn't terminate your call on my account,' Thane Addison offered with grim sarcasm.

'Khalil—Khalil Rashwan, he's leaving for Japan for a week or two,' she excused Khalil's call.

'Oh, good,' Thane drawled mockingly, then, his voice changing to granite, 'Perhaps now,' he said harshly, 'I might look forward to having your full and undivided attention during office hours.' And before she could retaliate that she considered his remark most unfair, he was straight away picking up from where he had left off in his dictation, and she was having to push her pencil at the gallop to catch up with him.

The rest of that Monday flashed by, with Joss so busy that she came to the firmest conclusion that she had had it easy working for Mr Edwards. Which fact made it a puzzle to her that, when Sami drove her back to her hotel that night, she should feel she would not have changed that day for a day back with Mr Edwards.

What that signified exactly, she had no idea, when after her dinner that night she went up to her room. Did it mean that she was so masochistic that she actually enjoyed working for that swine Thane Addison? He certainly kept her on her toes, but... Joss gave it up, and went to bed.

When Khalil Rashwan rang her at about three o'clock the next afternoon, she thought he had not gone to Japan after all. That was until he told her that he was phoning her from Japan!

'Was there something in particular you rang about?' she queried, thinking that to be calling from so far away must mean that his call had something to do with business.

'I rang particularly to hear your voice, Josslyn,' he told her warmly, and as Joss thought 'grief!' and that this situation looked to be getting out of hand, she was heartily glad that Thane Addison was out on a business meeting.

'That's very nice of you, Khalil,' she told him as evenly as she could, then went on to tell him, using all the tact at her command, that she would prefer it if he didn't ring her at her office.

The only trouble with that, she discovered as the week went by, was that Khalil took to ringing her every evening at her hotel. However, by the time Friday arrived she had grown more adept at tactfully handling the warmer of his comments.

By Friday, too, she was more adept at her work in Egypt, and felt more in the swing of what was trying to be achieved with the Osiris Corporation. The pace in that direction was starting to hot up, she realised as that Friday morning she sat at her typewriter finishing off a very rough draft of a contract which Richard Maybury and Seif Ismail had been in consultation over. She had started on the rough draft yesterday afternoon, and had worked late, but because there were so many pages of it she had not been able to complete it.

In actual fact, she was only coming to an end at twelve-thirty. Taking the last page out of her typewriter, she checked it over for mistakes, found none, and felt it couldn't be very much longer now before Thane Addison had reached his goal.

Collecting up the many sheets of the draft outline, she went into the other office, and as Thane looked up, she handed him the neat bundle of work.

'Is that all of it?' Thane enquired.

'Yes,' she replied, and felt a glow as he flicked through the pages, then said,

'You've done well.'

'I try,' she murmured drily.

'Then try to get me Yazid Rashwan; if he's free this afternoon I'll take this...' He broke off, something in her sudden change of expression stopping him. 'So what do you know that I don't?' he asked quietly.

Not a lot, she rather thought, though she did know that Yazid Rashwan was many miles away from Alexandria. 'Mr Rashwan's in Luxor,' she replied, and saw from the way Thane leaned back in his chair and steadily eyed her that he wanted more than that.

'And from where did you learn that titbit?' he enquired when she wasn't very forthcoming. 'Or should I say from whom?'

'Khalil told me.'

'He's back from Japan?'

Joss shook her head. 'He phoned...'

'When?' rapped Thane, and, dropping the work she had just given him down on his desk, he stood up, everything about him aggressive.

'Last night,' Joss told him quickly, then started to get cross herself—for heaven's sake, there was no need for Thane Addison to look the way he did! He should know by now that she wasn't likely to give away anything that was confidential to anyone!

'He phoned you last night, from Japan?' Thane demanded.

'Yes, he did!' she replied defiantly, refusing to be browbeaten.

From the narrowing of his eyes she knew that he neither liked her tone nor what she was saying. Nor did she like the cold thoughtful look that came to his eyes.

'It's not the first time he's rung you from Japan, is it?' he demanded.

'He rings every...' her voice faded as she saw the sudden jut of Thane's jaw. Then, 'No, it isn't!' she said shortly.

'In fact, he rings you at your hotel every night,' Thane documented, his aggression now out in the open. 'Every night, since you gave him the encouragement of promising to be here still when he gets back!'

Joss blinked at him in astonishment that he should remember so accurately the details of what she had said on that one and only phone call she had taken from Khalil in his presence. Then, 'I wasn't particularly encouraging him,' she tried to deny.

'I don't know what the hell else you'd call it!' he snarled, adding fiercely, 'But perhaps that's all right with you. Perhaps you don't mind that he's out to bed you! That his pursuit of you means...'

'It's not all right with me!' Joss cut in, outraged. 'I'm doing all I can to walk a middle line between not offending the man who's the son of the man you've said *is* the Osiris Corporation, while my paramount wish is to stay loyal to Beacon Oil. On top of that, I quite like Khalil, but,' she continued when a muscle jerked in Thane's temple, 'I've no intention whatsoever of going to bed with him.'

Thane took a pace away from her as she stormed to an end. Then he turned back and told her harshly, 'I'm not having all the effort I've put in on this job ruined by your telling Khalil Rashwan, in anything but diplomatic terms, to cool his ardour.'

'It won't come to that,' Joss replied as coolly as she could.

'Huh!' he scorned. 'If you really believe that then you're more naïve than you've a right to be.' Then, clearly not believing she was naïve at all, he thought for a moment, then came to a decision that left her little short of gaping. 'You'd better tell him when next he rings that, in his absence, you've become smitten with—me. Tell him...'

Joss's gasp of incredulity caused him to break off, and as astounded as she was by what she had just heard, she was nevertheless quick to erupt, 'I'll do nothing of the kind! Why,' she went on heatedly, even though it had nothing to do with what they were discussing, 'I don't even like you—much less fancy you!' she told him, and went to swing away from him.

She had reckoned, though, without the fact that Thane Addison did not care for people walking away from him in the middle of an argument. She was made to realise that fact, however, when he caught hold of her arm and swung her back to face him.

'Who the hell wants you to?' he roared, and all at once, as a sudden gleam entered his eyes, she realised that some new thought had just come to him when he breathed, 'Though to prove a point,' and the next she knew was that Thane Addison was hauling her into his arms.

Shock kept her motionless for about two seconds. That was all it took for him to have her close up against his body, and to place his lips over hers.

It was the feel of his warm, well-shaped mouth on her own, though, that startled Joss into an awareness of what was happening. And suddenly, she went wild. She aimed a kick at his shin, and missed. She tried to get a punch to his shoulder, only to find he had somehow pinioned her arms down by her sides. She twisted her head this way and that, and finally she managed to pull her head away from the close proximity of his.

'Let go of me!' she yelled, and when he wouldn't she tried to land another kick to his shins. That one missed too, and before she knew it, he had recaptured her mouth.

For perhaps another minute she fought to get free, then all at once, and quite unexpectedly, a new and different emotion from the outrage she had been seething with began to spurt into life. And she stopped fighting.

Quite when she began submitting, she did not know. Nor did she know quite when, instead of meekly submitting, as the fire he was igniting in her started to burn, and flame, she began to respond.

Indeed, she was barely conscious that she had begun to respond to the urges of her body until, with her body pressed close up against his, and with her arms wrapped tightly around him, she suddenly came to realise that it was he who was breaking their kiss, and not she! That it was he who was pushing her away from him—and not she who was pushing to try to get away from him.

Which, when it did dawn on her, left her more astounded than ever. Her unruffled front was well and truly routed and she was left in no way able to cope when, as his arms dropped to his sides, he mockingly surveyed her.

'Point proven, I think, Miss Harding,' he drawled. 'You don't have to like a man, much less fancy him. You turn on—without such niceties.'

Joss had been through several sharp emotions in the last ten minutes. She was suddenly visited by another—the emotion of violence. With her self-control shot, she had no chance of harnessing that violence, and in a flash her right hand had arced through the air.

Her hand stung from the impact of striking him a furious blow on the side of his face, but she was entirely unrepentant. Tossing her head in the air, she stormed back to her desk, snatched up her bag and sailed out of her office, and out of the building. The swine—she hoped it hurt!

CHAPTER FIVE

HALF AN HOUR later Joss was seated in a nearby hotel with a cup of coffee in front of her, and she was still fuming. It was lunchtime, but she was too furious to eat. How dared he? The pig of a man! She was glad she had hit him!

Another half-hour went by, during which time she had ordered another cup of coffee, and had hotly determined that he could keep his job. She didn't want it, she was going straight back to England. She might not have seen the Pyramids yet, but, Pyramids or no Pyramids, she was leaving.

When ten more minutes had passed and she had made no move to get going 'straight back to England', Joss realised that she had cooled down considerably from being so blazingly furious. She was still angry with Thane, but as another five minutes ticked by she started to think more with her head than with the heat of outraged emotion.

It was then that she began to realise that, by walking out on her job, she would be playing right into Thane Addison's hands. He'd just love that, wouldn't he? He'd had a down on female secretaries before she'd arrived. He'd just love to telex London and tell them to send another secretary out, doubly stressing this time that he insisted on a male.

Inside another two minutes Joss was thinking, like hell she'd leave! She thought back to how she had once determined she would stay—no matter how insulting Thane Addison was. And although she thought he could not get more insulting than to intimate, the way he had in his 'You turn on without such niceties', that she was anybody's, Joss started to dig her heels in. She wouldn't run, damn him. She was good at her work, she knew she was. Although this, she thought, as she got up, paid her bill and left the hotel, was a matter unconnected with her secretarial skills.

A taxi cruised by, a taxi which would have taken her to her hotel. She ignored it. She was not going to slink back to Beacon House, London, with her tail between her legs. No, she would not!

Halima was busy with a call on her switchboard when Joss, with her head tilted at a defiant angle, entered the Beacon Oil building. Joss smiled in her general direction and, with her heart suddenly banging against her ribs, went up the stairs to her own office.

The communicating door between the two offices was now closed, and as she reached her desk and stowed her bag she had no idea whether Thane was in or not. It did not take her very long to find out, however, for no sooner had she referred to her notepad and begun typing some work which had been held in abeyance while she typed the rough draft of the contract than the dividing door opened.

Stubbornly she refused to look up, but carried on with her typing. When the door closed again and Thane Addison did not come forward she guessed he was standing with his back against the door just watching her, and her fingers fumbled and she stopped typing.

Hoping to hide the sudden turmoil of her emotions under a cool front, she raised cool eyes and looked at him over the top of her typewriter. Instantly her glance was caught and held by him, and as an unbidden memory returned of the way she had pressed herself to him, had wrapped her arms around him—and had responded to his kisses—warm colour stained her cheeks.

She knew that his all-seeing glance had not missed the sudden flare of pink in her normally creamy skin, but all at once Joss was unconcerned with the irritating fact that, when she hadn't blushed in years, her blushing facility had chosen that moment to reassert itself. Because, when she had been too furious to consider the matter before, she was suddenly recalling how Paula Ingram was said to have thrown herself at Thane.

True, she doubted that Paula had attempted to fracture his cheekbone the way she had when she had hit him, but at that precise moment she started to get the feeling that the decision of whether she returned to England or stayed on in Egypt did not rest with her. She had been under no illusion before but that she would suffer the same ignominious fate as Paula Ingram if she ever came all 'female' over him. Again Joss recalled the way she had wrapped her arms around him, and suddenly she was certain that, like Paula, she was going to receive her marching orders.

Being certain of that, however, she still felt a very nasty jolt to see Thane Addison straighten from his casual stance by the door, and to hear him begin coolly, 'You'd better get back to your hotel and pack. I've——'

'That's most unfair!' she erupted hotly, immediately furious and on her feet as she refused to let him finish, and with no chance to hide the emotion she was feeling. 'You started it!' she raced on. 'I hit you because you— you... because of what you so vilely said,' she spluttered in her rage. 'You deserved it. You—' This time she wasn't allowed to finish.

'Whether I deserved your losing control of your fiery temper is neither here nor there!' he roared over the top of her voice, then commanded her toughly, 'Go and get your belongings together—'

'You swine!' Joss cried, the fiery temper he had spoken of outraged, as she slammed into her desk drawer for her bag. 'You utter swine!' she went on as she raced for the door.

She had the door open, but did not go through it. For suddenly he was speaking again, and all at once there was mockery in his voice. 'Cut the flattery, Miss Harding,' he drawled, 'or I may change my mind about the apartment I've found for you.'

Astounded, her jaw definitely dropping, she closed the door and turned back to him. 'You've found me—an apartment?' she asked, her temper flown, ashamed as she realised that if she'd let him finish what he'd started to say instead of going off half cocked, she'd have had no reason to lose her temper.

'Go and pack,' was his answer.

Joss moved into the furnished apartment which Thane had found for her that Friday night, and spent Saturday and Sunday thoroughly enjoying her new abode. Hotel living was all right as a stopgap, she mused, but her apartment was cosier and much more like home.

There were moments, though, when she would stop in the middle of being thrilled to bits to be in her new home, to feel overcome with guilt at the quick way she had wrongly assumed what she had.

She had been wrong to accuse Thane of being unfair, she acknowledged, totally wrong. She had seen enough by now of the way Thane worked to know that he was about the fairest person she had ever come across. He would not have needed her reminder that 'he had started it' to know that it would be unfair to dismiss her for something which he had instigated. And she, she realised a little unhappily, should have known better.

In her defence, though, she had been upset, and he was the cause. That still didn't make it right, she owned honestly, and accepted that he was due an apology from her for having so unfairly thought what she had.

In facing honestly that she owed him an apology, however, Joss found that she could not as honestly take out her reactions to Thane's kisses and dissect them. He, and his expertise, must take the blame there, she decided, and swiftly turned her thoughts to the fact that as her stay in Egypt could not be for much longer now, for the short remainder of her stay Thane had moved her out of the hotel and into an apartment.

She doubted that it would bother him one way or another that she might be happier living in an apartment, but realised, when thinking about it, that since in every thriving business all expenditure had to be accounted for, even for the short time remaining, it was probably more economical for her to switch from an expensive hotel and into furnished accommodation.

Joss hadn't given thought to how she would get to work, but, thinking that there was no time like the present to find out, she left her apartment at her usual half-past eight on Monday. She smiled at the concierge as she passed him, and went into the outside sunlight— to see none other than the faithful Sami.

'Good morning, madam.' He beamed his gentle smile.

'Good morning, Sami,' she greeted him cheerfully, and so started a week where Halima told her that Mr Addison was already closeted with Richard Maybury in conference, and where when she reached her office, her first telephone call of the day was from Khalil Rashwan in Japan.

'Why didn't you tell me that you were checking out of your hotel?' he asked at once. 'I have been trying to reach you by telephone!' he exclaimed, and sounded quite distraught.

'I moved into an apartment on Friday,' Joss told him cheerfully, having by then discovered that Khalil had a tendency to be overdramatic, but soon settled down if she didn't take too much notice.

'Then you must give me your telephone number at once,' he declared.

'I...' Joss broke off, as only then did it dawn on her that she couldn't remember having seen a phone in the apartment. 'I don't think I've got one,' she told him. When later the call was ended, she put the phone down, knowing that for the short time she would be there, there seemed little point in doing as he'd requested and having a phone installed at her apartment immediately.

From there a week followed where Khalil, while apologising for ringing her at the office, still rang her most days—having a few more dramatics one day when he fretted that he would not be back in Egypt as soon as he'd thought. Joss went out for a meal with Chad Woollams one night during that week, and learned that he was recently divorced and trying to cover the fact that it still hurt. While at the office, she started to feel a definite 'buzz' in the negotiating department.

Not that things were going without a hitch. So many amendments had been made to the rough draft which she had typed that the whole thing had to be done again.

When that week rolled to a close, she felt exhausted, but as if she at last had something to get her teeth into. She quickly recovered, however, and was glad to repay Grace and Richard Maybury's hospitality by having them to her apartment for dinner.

And then, before she could turn around, it was Monday again. 'Hello, Sami,' she greeted the Egyptian driver as she left her apartment, and by the time she reached her office she was geared up to start another week.

She had no sooner reached her office, however, than Thane Addison came through the open communicating door. He looked at her for long unspeaking moments, and then, just when she was expecting to get her ears singed for something she had done or had forgotten to do, 'Good morning,' he grunted, then told her, 'I've got to go to Cairo.'

'I'll find something to do,' she murmured, knowing that she wouldn't have to look very far, though lord knew where the vast amounts of paperwork she daily got through came from.

'Hmph,' he grunted, his sense of humour clearly very Monday-morningish, and was halfway back into his office when he stopped, turned around, looked at her, then told her, 'Stop looking—you're coming to Cairo with me.'

Joss had been on the Cairo to Alexandria road before, only then it had been late at night. This time when Thane drove the reverse journey from Alexandria to Cairo, it was daylight, and she was able to see, with the sun shining brightly overhead, that it was indeed desert on either side of the two parallel roads.

Occasionally there were signs of greenery, and now and then quite a bit of vegetation, but only to soon change to desert again. The journey was uneventful, however, with Thane as far as she could gather concentrating his thoughts on business matters and preferring her to be silent. He had very little to say to her at any rate, but she didn't mind that. Somehow all seemed right with her world, and she experienced a feeling of contentment.

That feeling of contentment was still with her when they reached Beacon House. She was pleased to see Baz

Barton again, who, after respectfully greeting her boss, suddenly beamed her a smile and seemed delighted to see her.

'Joss!' he cried, and asked, 'How goes it?'

'Cooper in his office?' Thane Addison cut in crisply before she could answer, and before she knew it she was whisked into Malcolm Cooper's office and the door was closed, and they were getting down to business.

In actuality, Joss couldn't have said that she considered her presence very necessary at the meeting between Thane Addison and Malcolm Cooper, but, remembering how on her first day of working for him he had told her to keep her eyes and ears open, she absorbed as much of the highly technical talk as she could, and took notes whenever she was requested to do so.

When later on Thane became fully occupied in sifting through some complicated figure work with Malcolm, Joss went from the office to see if there was any coffee going. It was then that she met Oma, Halima's Cairo counterpart. Oma spoke English every bit as well as Halima, but, with Baz Barton wanting to monopolise Joss, Joss did not get much of a chance for a conversation with her.

'Chad Woollams has all the luck,' he told her at one point.

'Why?' she asked innocently.

'He's based in Alexandria,' he replied, and at her look of enquiry he told her, 'So are you.' He grinned, which caused her to have to smile, and then the door to Malcolm Cooper's office opened and Thane stood there.

She caught his disgruntled look, and for a moment she thought that something had been amiss with the figures he had been looking at. She realised, when he went striding to the outer door and held the door open for her, that it wasn't that he was disgruntled but that he must have a lot on his mind.

'Bye!' she called to Oma and Baz, and to Malcolm who had followed Thane out. Then she went quickly to where Thane was standing. We're coming on, she thought; at one time he wouldn't have held the door open for her but would have left her to sprint after him.

That, or have snarled 'Come!' or some such order, she thought whimsically as they reached his car and she stood waiting for him to unlock it. Such whimsy, however, brought a smile to her face.

Though she had no idea that she was smiling until she heard Thane sharply challenging, 'Something amusing you?'

On any other day, such fierceness would have made her rise up swiftly. But the strange feeling of contentment was still with her, and for once since she had known him Joss felt not the smallest inclination to flare up in return.

So, meeting the fierce glare of his look serenely, she suddenly smiled. 'I had coffee,' she told him. 'You didn't.'

'Get in,' he grunted as he turned his key and all four doors unlocked.

Joss bent her head to 'get in', but not before she had glimpsed that his mouth, though looking severely repressed, was definitely trying to pull upwards at the corners.

They had been on the Cairo to Alexandria road for about an hour and a half when Thane pulled off the road and turned into a modern single-storeyed restaurant. And Joss could not have been more pleased about that. Not for herself, but for him. It was, in her opinion, more than time he had a rest.

'Hungry?' he asked, as he escorted her into the restaurant.

'Yes,' she replied truthfully, for by then it was way past lunchtime.

To her pleasure, however, instead of getting back into the car and continuing on their way once their meal was eaten, Thane suggested that they stretch their legs by taking a short stroll along the paths which separated neatly kept lawns. She paused for a short while when they came to a small budgerigar aviary, and was pleased when Thane did not seem impatient to move on. From there they moved to look at some hens which were kept in an immaculate wire-netted enclosure which was complete with house and run.

It was as they strolled back to the car, however, that Joss realised, without being able to put her finger on any specific reason why, that she was quite enjoying the day. Which in turn caused her to realise that, with Thane being at his most affable since she had known him, it was more than high time that she apologised to him. Her apology for accusing him of unfairness when he had never meant to dismiss her was long overdue. Not that she would apologise for hitting him, she thought without heat, as he started up the car and they got on their way again. He had deserved that.

'I never did—er—say—I was sorry,' she began while the idea was upon her, though having not realised, as she faltered, how difficult it was to bring the subject up.

'For your having had a coffee back in the Cairo office and leaving me to die of thirst?' he queried, and she loved that note of humour in his voice.

'No,' she owned with a laugh, and was serious when she added, 'for thinking you unfair.'

'Apology accepted,' he said lightly, and Joss's feeling of inner contentment expanded. She was not quite sure how she felt, however, when, clearly having thought back to what had triggered off her accusing him of being unfair—she having hit him for his remarks, and what had led up to those remarks—he enquired casually, 'Is Khalil Rashwan still ringing you every evening from Japan?'

His voice had remained light, Joss noted, as she told him, 'No,' and added, since he obviously didn't know, 'There's no phone in the apartment you found for me.' She was on the point of realising that he could not know that Khalil rang her most days at the office, since by pure coincidence he had been elsewhere when those calls had come through, when after sifting through her reply, he suddenly had another question.

'He knows you've checked out of the hotel, though?' he asked, his tone abrupt, all lightness suddenly gone.

'He rang me—at the office—when the hotel told him that I no longer lived there,' she was forced to confess.

'So he's taken to ringing you *every day* at the office?' Thane barked, and as storm clouds threatened, every bit of Joss's feeling of inner contentment vanished.

'Not every day!' she answered sharply, and, since she felt that she had done nothing wrong, 'But most days!' she told him defiantly.

'A fact which you were going to keep to yourself!' Thane snarled.

'It's got nothing to do with work!' she erupted.

'Yes, it has!' roared Thane, and while the only complaint she could see he had cause for was that she was taking those calls on the office phone during office hours—and surely nobody was that mean-minded these days?—he was telling her curtly, 'While I'm in charge of this Egyptian project I want to know everything that goes on. If I'm to have facts down to the nth degree at my fingertips, I want to know every time anyone from Osiris makes a move. Your first loyalty, Miss Harding,' he told her harshly, 'while you're employed by Beacon Oil, is to me!'

'You *are* unfair!' she exploded, not taking kindly to being so trounced. 'Khalil and I are just—friends. Work doesn't come into it!'

'Don't be so bloody stupid!' Thane thundered. 'He's the son of the man who runs Osiris, isn't he?'

Joss didn't answer. Feeling furious to be called stupid—bloody stupid at that—she stared out of the side window. From then on until they reached Alexandria, she said not another word.

By then, though, she had simmered down as she remembered that Yazid Rashwan had, more than once, effectively gummed up the works of getting final draft contract details agreed upon. She knew that Khalil was his only son, and very dear to him. Which made her wonder then—as Thane all too clearly had wondered—whether, should Khalil have cause to complain about her for some unknown reason, might not his father—even at this late stage—change his mind about what was a multi-million-pound deal.

It was something of a pill to swallow that for a second time she had unjustly accused Thane of being unfair, but as he parked his car near to Beacon House Joss could not bring herself to apologise. She was still smarting from being called bloody stupid. Besides, she had apologised once that day—once, in her opinion, was enough.

She was still of that opinion when Sami drove her back to her apartment that night. Nor was she feeling in any friendlier frame of mind towards Thane Addison when Sami drove her to the office the next morning. Though when, included this time, she went with him to a meeting with Yazid Rashwan to take any notes that might be required, she could not help but admire Thane as she witnessed at first hand the way he dealt with each sticking point as it cropped up. Somehow she had imagined a troubleshooter to be a person who went in there with guns blazing, but it wasn't like that at all. There was no doubting that Thane could be tough when the occasion demanded it. But she was staggered to witness his seemingly endless patience, his willingness to take apart piece by piece the tiniest obstacle. Thane's diplomacy, too, was of the highest, she saw—that diplomacy being much in evidence when he himself refused to yield ground.

All in all, Joss clearly saw that morning why Thane Addison had been sent in when all other efforts had failed. When at the end of that meeting a definite breakthrough had been made, she could not have been more thrilled.

She spent that afternoon taking down page after page of highly confidential matter. She felt then that she could forgive Thane anything that, after losing his temper with her the way he had yesterday, he still obviously trusted her—and her loyalty. For not only had he taken her with him to that meeting this morning, but he was now quoting figures to her which any competitor would give their eye teeth to get hold of.

Knowing that her work was wanted urgently, she worked late that night, but had still typed only half of it when at eight o'clock Thane, who was also working, came into her office and told her briefly, 'That's ample for today.'

She spent all Wednesday morning in finishing off her typing, and, while being aware that the document was not fully complete, she handed her typing to Thane, who then summoned Richard Maybury to his office. When at four o'clock Thane called her in, he was alone, but had the work she had handed him before him. It was clear to her then that he and Richard Maybury had been sifting through it with a fine-tooth comb.

'Can you work late again this evening?' he asked, the fact that he had *asked* a plus, even if she was fully aware that he'd have something caustic to say if she replied that she couldn't.

'Of course,' she told him promptly, and, sensing that it was connected with the work she had laboured over, 'Is there something wrong?' she asked seriously, though she did not see how there could be, since she had double-checked her work.

'Couldn't be more right,' Thane answered, and over the next couple of hours he dictated material which was to be inserted into the work she had been engaged upon.

Joss, who by then knew the concise way in which Thane constructed his business sentences, knew immediately that he had asked, and taken, Richard Maybury's legal opinion on certain of the clauses. But the whole of the while they were working, a picture was building up, so that at the end of that two hours Joss, whose intellect had not stayed idle, had started to tingle.

So much so that when Thane had dictated the last full stop, she had grown quite excited. She tried to remain calm, and thought she might have succeeded, but she could do nothing about the shining look of elation in her eyes when, raising her head, she just had to say, 'That's it—isn't it? The contract, I mean! You've done it! You've...' Her voice faded as she caught his intent glance on her.

Then he was leaning back in his chair and telling her, 'True,' and all at once he smiled the most wonderful smile and suddenly, crazily, Joss wanted to kiss him. Then Thane was flicking a glance at his watch and, telling her to make two copies, was adding, 'And now I must make tracks for the airport.'

'Airport?' She gave herself a mental shake and asked in surprise, 'You're—meeting a plane?'

'I'm catching one—I'm flying to England,' he told her, and all at once her heart plummeted—he had finished his work; he wasn't coming back!

'You—er—must be exceedingly pleased at what you've achieved,' she hoisted her unflappable front aloft to tell him, and knew unbounded pleasure suddenly when, after pausing for a moment, he smiled a second time.

'I won't consider my side of the job done until I see Yazid Rashwan's initials next to mine on that preliminary contract,' he told her, indicating the work she had in her hands. He was on his feet when he told her that Richard Maybury was working late too, and would give her a lift home. Then, having thought of everything, it seemed, he was giving her face a steady scrutiny and telling her, 'See you when I get back,' as he went striding to the door. At the door, however, he turned, looked at her again, then said quietly, 'Bye, Joss.'

For an age after he had gone, Joss stayed staring at the door he had closed after him. She knew that she was going to miss him, but it was not until several minutes later that she was able to pull herself together and to realise that to think for one moment that she was going to miss him must surely mean she had been out in the sun too long.

She finally left Thane's office and returned to her own where, glancing down at the new dictation he had given her, plus amendments and insertions to the contract, she realised that it totalled up to two days' work. She had better get started.

The next hour flew by, but she had barely dented her workload when Richard Maybury came up to tell her that he was calling it a day. 'Can I put my work in your safe?' she asked him as she began to get her papers together.

'Of course,' he replied, and a short while later, with her confidential work locked in his safe, he gave her a lift to her apartment.

It took Joss a long time to get to sleep that night. Again and again as she closed her eyes she would find her thoughts on Thane Addison, who was winging his way through the late night on his five-hour flight to England. Most oddly, as she assumed that he probably had a board meeting to attend in the morning, she wondered if he would get a chance to catch some sleep on that flight.

A moment later she was asking herself, good heavens, what did she care? In any case, she had worked for the man—he was superhuman—he probably didn't need any sleep.

For a while she forced her thoughts away from him and dwelt instead on the man who had posed many difficulties for Thane on the road to reaching this preliminary contract stage. She had been working in Egypt for just over three weeks now, and if she had gleaned anything in that time it was that, for all Yazid Rashwan had not made reaching agreement easy, having at last reached agreement over the contract, he would stick to it. He was the same type of man of honour as was Thane Addison, and though small changes might later be made before the main contract was drawn up, once both men had set their initials to the preliminary agreement both, she felt, would consider its major content binding.

Thoughts of Yazid Rashwan and of how everything would work for the mutual benefit and future prosperity of both the Osiris Corporation and Beacon Oil were far from Joss just before sleep at last arrived. For by then she was longer able to keep at bay the memory of the crazy and most extraordinary emotion that had taken her when, realising what Thane had pulled off, she had experienced the urge to kiss him.

Grief! He'd have loved that, wouldn't he? She could just see him now, telling her, as he had told her within the first half-hour of their meeting, something about having enough problems '...without having to take time out to discipline another member of staff who takes it into her head to go all female on me'. Joss pulled the covers over her head and went to sleep.

Thursday was a day where she typed herself to a standstill. Friday was very much the same, and she finally pushed her typewriter back from her at around three o'clock. She then set about checking and rechecking the contract she had just spent two days in getting into shape, and forgave herself for her feeling of pride as she finally placed the impeccable end result in a folder of thin cardboard. Then the phone on her desk rang, and it was Chad Woollams.

'Haven't you got a home to go to?' he joked.

Swiftly Joss looked at her watch. She saw that it was ten past five. 'Tell Sami to hang on,' she replied, 'I've just got to give Richard something for the safe, then I'll be ready to...'

'Sami's still here, Richard isn't.'

'He isn't?'

'He said something about Grace wanting to take a trip to Aswan this weekend, so he shot off early,' Chad explained.

Joss thought for a second—there were two safes in the building, but she had a key to neither. I knew I'd brought that leather document wallet with me for something, she mused. 'I'll be with you in five minutes,' she told Chad, realising that he was waiting to lock up. Putting down the phone, she opened a drawer in her desk and took out the leather document case that, in four weeks of her working in Egypt, had not had an airing.

Perhaps she was being over-cautious, she contemplated when, with the bulging wallet in her hand, she left her office. The likelihood of any of their competitors forcing entry into Beacon House seemed remote, but industrial espionage was a fact in big business and not fallacy, and she hadn't broken her back setting down specific details and figures only to have them stolen. As an added precaution, as well as the two copies of the contract, her notes and shorthand notepad were in the wallet too.

Once Sami had dropped her off, Joss made her way up to her apartment and relaxed with a cup of tea. Then, feeling somewhat revived, she went and had a shower and washed her hair. She decided to let her hair dry naturally and ran a comb through it, and, clad in her housecoat, went into her kitchen and made herself a snack.

She had eaten her meal and cleared away, and was in the throes of wondering if she should write another letter home while considering that since there couldn't be very much more for her to do in Egypt now that she would probably arrive in England before her letter, when someone rang her doorbell.

She knew with confidence that none but the most presentable would get past the concierge, and so, checking only to see that the housecoat she had on was securely fastened, she went and opened the door a tiny way. And, as her heart started to race idiotically as she saw Thane so unexpectedly standing there, she pulled the door open wider.

'Th...Mr Addison!' she exclaimed. 'When did you get back?'

His answer was to study her from the top of her newly washed blonde head to the tips of her mule-clad but otherwise bare feet. Then he smiled a slow smile, a warm smile, then drawled softly, 'I agree—it is time you used my first name.'

'Come in,' she invited, and suddenly became conscious that her newly washed hair was fluffy, and that she hadn't a scrap of make-up on, and that she needed a moment—or several—to get herself together.

Having turned away from him, she turned back to look at him as he followed her into her sitting-room. He seemed strangely dear to her then, this tall, broad-shouldered, grey-eyed man, whom she was beginning to acknowledge she had missed seeing this last two days.

But while she was busy in stoutly contradicting any ridiculous notion that he was dear to her, or that she had missed him, for goodness' sake, she saw that his eyes were travelling around her sitting-room.

'You're quite settled here?' he enquired when his eyes had done a full circuit and had come to rest on her face.

'Oh yes,' she replied, refraining from telling him that she wouldn't have a chance to settle and that she'd be back in England before too long. Though, since this was the first time that he had bothered to put the question at all since he had found her the apartment, she gave him a friendly smile and said, 'Can I offer you a drink?'

It was a cause for relief that he opted for a cup of coffee; her alcohol supply was less than limited. She left him in her sitting-room while she went into the kitchen, and cogitated on whether she should go and change out of her housecoat. She made the coffee wondering if he would think her stupid if she did change—since he was only going to stay for as long as it took for him to drink his coffee. She then got totally cross with herself to think that when she had always been in charge of herself, and able to make positive decisions, she should suddenly, for some obscure reason, have turned into such an indecisive creature.

When she took the tray of coffee into her sitting-room she was still clad in her housecoat and, having given herself a brief lecture, was decidedly in charge of herself.

As yet she had no idea why Thane had called, but since she felt that it could not have been to specifically ask her if she was settled there, she supposed he would tell her when he was ready. In the meantime she poured two cups of coffee, and, handing him one of them, enquired, 'How was England?'

'Raining,' he replied, and studied his cup for a second, then raised piercing grey eyes to look into hers and question offhandedly, 'Anxious to get back?'

'To the rain?' she laughed.

'To the man friend?' he answered.

'There's no one in particular,' she owned lightly.

'Fergus Perrott?' he queried, making her blink that he should have remembered Fergus's name after all these weeks.

'My girlfriend Abby is more interested in Fergus than I am,' Joss informed him, and somehow found herself telling him about the theatre group, her non-acting role in it, and how she had come to be in Fergus's company that night after the telex had come in from Cairo.

'How fortunate for us,' Thane commented when she had come to an end, and as she stared at him to realise that he must be saying, in a roundabout way, that he was pleased it was she who had been sent out to Egypt, he suddenly smiled.

Again Joss was taken by his smile, but she had just been reminded that he hadn't wanted a female secretary at all, and certainly not one who went all female on him. She decided then that the only way she had missed him was not having him around to bark out his commands over the last two days.

'Do I take it from that, that a female secretary isn't so bad after all?' she murmured, as she took a sip of coffee.

'Talking of work,' Thane easily ignored her question, 'Yazid Rashwan was on the phone to me as soon as I got in.'

'Everything's still all right, isn't it?' she asked urgently.

'Of course,' he replied, and with the confidence of a man who knew his job, and who also knew he had done his job well, 'Once Yazid and I have initialled that contract then as far as he and I are concerned—given that both our legal offices will make minor adjustments out of love of jargonese—the crude oil contract will be in the bag.'

Joss was about to ask if she should congratulate him now, when she suddenly remembered something. 'Oh, I've had to bring both copies of the contract home with me!' she exclaimed quickly.

'You have?' he queried, his grey eyes on her alive expression.

'I didn't have time to put them in the safe before Richard left tonight,' she explained, and felt warmed right to the core of her at Thane's reply.

'My fault,' he accepted full responsibility, and then, endorsing how much he trusted her, 'I was on my way to the airport when I remembered I'd meant to leave you the safe key,' he told her, which compliment made her forget her intention to go and get the document wallet for him.

'You were rather busy that day,' she excused his small lapse of memory in masterly understatement.

'*We* were,' he corrected, and the fact that he had not overlooked that she had worked hard that day too made her feel good inside. Then Thane was going on, 'As I was saying, Yazid telephoned me a short while ago—he's invited us to his home in Luxor for a few days.'

'Luxor!' she exclaimed, and the contracts had gone completely from her mind as what Thane had just said penetrated. *'Us?'* she questioned, and all at once started to feel excited at the prospect. Though her excitement swiftly dimmed as she saw from Thane's sudden frown that she must have got it wrong somewhere. 'Not us?' she queried.

'I've agreed we'll go to Luxor,' he replied, a certain coolness starting to show in his manner, 'but have had to decline the invitation to stay in his home.'

'Had to?' queried Joss, not quite understanding why. 'Because—it wouldn't be right from a business point of view?' she queried, and received an irritated look for her trouble.

'Once that contract is initialled Yazid and I will both be on the same side businesswise,' he told her impatiently. Sarcasm had entered his tones as he added, 'In case you didn't know—his son will be home.'

The change in Thane from the good-humoured man he had been to the sarcastic brute he now was was as confusing to Joss as what he was saying. 'What's Khalil being home got to do with——?' It was as far as she got.

'Where the hell have you been all your life?' Thane blasted explosively. And while she sat and blinked at the sudden anger in him, 'Confound it, woman,' he roared, 'can't you see he's panting for you?'

'Of course he isn't!' she burst in hotly, only to be shouted down.

'Of course he is!' he barked. Then suddenly he quietened, and started to look a shade incredulous. 'You can't see it, can you?' he asked. And while Joss stared wide-eyed at him, 'Are you as innocent as you look?' he questioned, and when she had no intention whatsoever of confirming that for him, she then had more evidence that he was never content until all questions had been answered to his satisfaction. 'Saints preserve us ... are you a virgin?' he demanded.

'What's that got to do with anything?' Joss suddenly erupted, not liking the feeling that she was being taken to task for something that was totally outside of business.

Watching him stormily, she saw his faintly incredulous look change to one of complete astonishment. She knew then that he had read all the confirming truth he needed in her reply. It was all there in his exclaimed, 'Oh, my godfathers!'

'And what am I supposed to gather from that?' she asked shortly, not liking him very much just then.

She discovered that he wasn't liking her very much either when, on his feet and clearly about to leave, he stayed to snarl angrily, 'For two pins I'd take your virginity myself, get that out of the way, then throw you to the wolves!'

'When I want that sort of a doubtful treat from you,' Joss retorted furiously, rocketing to her feet too in her rage, 'I'll let you know!'

Toe to toe they stood breathing fire at each other as hostilely Joss glared into the furnace of grey eyes in which she read that it would give him something of a pleasure to strangle her. Then, while she was feeling that she wouldn't at all mind setting about him, suddenly the humour of the situation got to her. At that self-same moment she saw Thane's lips twitch. Then, simultaneously, and while all the odds were against it, they both burst out laughing.

Who moved first as their laughter faded, she had no idea, but suddenly, as Thane looked at her, and as she stared quietly up at him, she found she was in his arms.

Gently he lowered his head and kissed her. Then his arms had fallen from her and he was going towards the door. 'I'll call for you in the morning,' he said as he reached it.

'You'll—call for me?' she queried, feeling somewhat bemused and not very clever in the brain department.

'I did say,' he murmured, 'we're going to Luxor.'

He had gone by the time Joss came out of her bemused state. Suddenly, though, a slow smile appeared on her face. She was going to Luxor—tomorrow—with him! Ten minutes later she realised that he had intimated that it might be for a few days. Joss thought she had better go and pack.

CHAPTER SIX

JOSS was up early on Saturday morning. Though she could hardly put the blame for that on the fact that she didn't know at what time Thane might arrive and might, if he intended to drive the five hundred or so miles she calculated it was to Luxor, call for her at the crack of dawn.

She had been wide awake when light started to appear in the night sky at about five-thirty and, having slept badly, she left her bed. She realised that the most probable cause for the fact that she had barely slept must be a little excitement. She had remembered during the night having read how, only recently, archaeologists had dug out some centuries-old statues from an underwater dig at the Temple of Luxor. And she was actually going to Luxor!

She was bathed and dressed in no time, and had remembered again Thane's gentle kiss on her mouth. But she didn't want to dwell on that. It had no special significance, anyway. Not that she had wanted it to have. Good heavens, it had been no more than a moment of empathy after their shared laughter.

Determinedly she put the memory from her, and decided it was more being told she was going to Luxor than Thane's kiss that had taken from her head every thought of giving him the copies of the contract. She cogitated for quite some while about whether she should pack the document case with the clothes she would take, but in the end she opted to carry it. It could well be that they would be going by train to Luxor, or maybe they would fly there. She had no idea which mode of transport they would use, but for security she decided she wanted that important leather wallet where she could see it.

When it came to what clothes she should pack, Joss had been in another quandary. The only suitcase she had with her was a large one—a trifle big for the 'few days' which Thane had spoken of them being away. On thinking about it, however, she saw no point, since she had plenty of room in the case, in not taking an item of clothing to cover every occasion.

She glanced round her apartment, took in the fact that it was neat and tidy to come back to, and sat down to wait for Thane, wishing she had thought to ask him at what time he would call.

It was half-past eight when, just as she had taken another look at her watch, someone rang her doorbell. Instantly she was out of her chair, and had taken a few steps towards the outer door when she suddenly stopped dead. Inexplicably, crazily, she suddenly felt over-whelmingly shy to see Thane again.

Grief! she snorted mentally, unable to remember ever feeling this way before. My giddy aunt! Just because he had gently kissed her! She was twenty-three, for goodness' sake!

Having given herself a swift and hurried lecture along the lines that she was not some awkward schoolgirl, Joss went to the door. As she remembered how amicably they had parted last night, a friendly smile curved her mouth as she pulled open the door.

'You took your time!' grunted Thane, and her smile swiftly departed, and she swallowed down the hot rush of words to tell him that if he felt like that about it he could go to Luxor by himself.

He was her boss, she remembered in time as she looked up at his unfriendly, unsmiling, I-hate-female-secretaries face. It might be a Saturday, but she had never considered herself a strictly nine-to-five Monday-to-Friday secretary, so she stepped back from the door and picked up her case, document wallet and shoulder-bag. 'I forgot what time you said you'd be here,' she told him prettily, feeling fairly certain that he would recall that he had kept that piece of information to himself.

He gave her a cutting look and with a snide, 'Travelling light today, I see!' he wrested the large suitcase from her grip and went down the stairs, leaving her to secure her flat.

Joss was again thinking him a pig of a man by the time she joined him in his car. She'd be damned if she'd explain that at such short notice as last night she had had no chance to go out and purchase anything smaller in the case line, she fumed, as they drove away. In fact, she decided as a short while later she realised that they were making for the airport, she'd be damned if she'd say anything to the man.

That her silence throughout the drive to the airport bothered him not a scrap was obvious by the way he totally ignored her. Indeed, he had parked the car and had her case in one hand, his much smaller case in his other hand, while at the same time he effortlessly managed to hang on to his briefcase too, when he addressed her at all. And that was only to rap a terse, 'You've got the contract with you?' as he eyed her document wallet.

'Both copies!' she retorted, and, since he hadn't a free hand to receive it, she was—while stifling the urge to hit him over the head with it—still holding on to it when they entered the airport building.

They had some time to wait at the airport, for as well as airport security being very strict, their plane was late. The flight to Luxor, however, was uneventful. Though with Thane burying his head in some paperwork extracted from his briefcase, Joss had time and space in which to wonder what happened in the night-time hours to turn him from the good-humoured man who had left her apartment last night to the bad-tempered brute he was this morning.

It didn't take her very long to find the answer. Nothing had happened. When had he ever been any different? Hadn't he always been the same: pleasant or nearly so one minute, then, without reason as far as she could see, coming on all stroppy with her.

Let him get on with it! she fumed, then fell to wondering, as she had during her wakeful hours last night, if he had really refused Yazid Rashwan's invitation for them to stay in his house on account of Khalil's being there. She felt sure that he must be wrong about Khalil panting for her, though that was beside the point, the point being—had Thane really risked offending Mr Rashwan by turning down his invitation to stay in his home? Had he really risked offending the Egyptian's proud honour?

Joss was still finding it incredible that Thane might have risked putting the contract he had laboured so hard and long over in jeopardy, as the plane started to descend at Luxor. From what she had witnessed, she had seen that both Thane and Yazid had a very great mutual respect for each other, a respect that bordered on friendship, so it wasn't so surprising perhaps that at the end of their work Yazid Rashwan should, from that feeling of friendship, extend the invitation.

Thane, in his business dealings, had a plentiful supply of tact, of course—not that he ever wasted any of it on her. The plane had landed when Joss realised that she must have got it wrong somewhere. For knowing Thane as she did, and the importance of this contract as she did, she felt certain that if it was a choice between risking the contract or risking her, then, to use his own charming expression, she'd be the one who would be thrown to the wolves.

Joss found Luxor a good deal warmer than Alexandria, and was glad she was wearing lightweight cotton clothes. She still had charge of her document wallet as, by taxi, she and Thane left the airport.

Luxor was as bustling and as busy as Alexandria, she observed, though a good deal more touristy. She wondered if she would have a chance to see the Temple of Luxor, but began to doubt it. She had been in Egypt nearly a month—and hadn't seen the Pyramids yet!

The taxi drew up outside a smart hotel, and, with Thane being such a terse brute, Joss was human enough to hope, when with supreme confidence he strode up to the reception desk, that they would tell him they were so busy with the tourists that there wasn't a room to be had.

They said nothing of the kind, of course. 'You have two rooms for me, name of Addison,' he told the receptionist. And while he went through the checking-in formalities, Joss realised that not only must he have telephoned in advance, but that men like him would always get a hotel room. Even if the hotel was so fully booked that the manager had to move out, Thane Addison would get a room, she thought sourly.

'I'll get a porter to take your cases up,' the receptionist said when the formalities were completed, and Thane turned to Joss.

'I've got a busy afternoon,' he told her shortly. 'Get yourself some lunch and...' He broke off, and as he seemed to study her face for a second, she caught a glimpse of something less harsh enter his expression—or thought she did, but knew herself mistaken when in the next second it vanished, and he was telling her crisply, 'We're dining at Yazid Rashwan's home this evening— you'd better rest this afternoon.'

Without a word Joss turned away and went with the porter. Thanks for telling me I look a wreck! she mutinied. She didn't want to *rest*, she didn't need to *rest*. Damn it, why did that man continually upset her so?

A moment later she was of the view that it wasn't that he upset her in particular, but that *he* would try the patience of a saint. She put thoughts of him out of her head when, not condescending to witness that his luggage was taken to his room, he had left her to do it.

'*Shokran gaezilaen,*' she thanked the porter, handing him the expected tip which she had discovered was very much part and parcel of the Egyptian way of life, and, observing that she and Thane had rooms next to each other, she checked that his smaller case was deposited inside one of them, and claimed the other.

Wretched man, she rebelled, and, Saturday or no Saturday, it was her considered opinion that if he was working, he should want her to work too—not *rest*!

That, though, was before she recalled that he hadn't said he was working but that 'I've got a busy afternoon'. Oh, to hell with him, she fumed, and, as visions of him having a busy non-working afternoon started to crowd her head, she rang room service. It was nearing three o'clock when she ordered an omelette and a salad, and decided to unpack.

Having newly discovered that they were dining at Yazid Rashwan's home that evening, Joss was pleased with her last-minute thought both in England and in Alexandria to pack one floor-length gown that would cover any formal, semi-formal, or just about any occasion. Shaking out the cream silk with its muted splodges of nasturtium, lemon and orange, she thought it would fit the bill nicely.

The dress had a deep but decorous neckline from which a four-inch flounce fell in soft folds, those folds repeated where the material flared softly from hip to hem. Its sleeves were elbow-length and the cut was such that it showed off her slender waist admirably. Joss knew she looked good in the dress that appeared quite simple but had cost so much that, without the cheque her parents had given her for her birthday last year, she would have had to think twice about such self-indulgence.

Her unpacking did not take long, and she wandered out on to her balcony and for a while was lost in wonder at the view. For there across the road from her hotel flowed the lifeline of Egypt, the Nile. Watching, she saw a crowded ferry make its way to the other side of the river's bank, where lush green grasses and tall date palms formed a foreground to the majestic and arid red-gold Theban Hills.

Somewhat in awe of the magnificence before her, she stayed on her balcony, turning her head this way and that, just absorbing all that was spread out as far as the eye could see. Then the man from room service arrived with her meal.

Since there were a couple of rattan chairs and a table out on the balcony, there was no question but that the balcony was where she would eat. She had been sitting tucking into her meal for some minutes, however, while gazing at the date palm, still with a cluster of unharvested dates hanging down on a level with her balcony, when it suddenly occurred to her that since the date palm went way past her balcony, and since she was on the sixth floor, then, incredibly—how tall was this particular tree for heaven's sake?

She never did get to calculate the answer, for, annoyingly, as though determined to upset her, thoughts of

Thane Addison and his cantankerous manner that day started to edge in.

Drat the man, she thought irritably, her moments of peace from him not long enough. But, her meal finished, her mood of happy discovery gone, she left the balcony and decided to change, deciding at the same time to thumb her nose to his 'You'd better rest this afternoon', and go out. When had it ever bothered him if she went on till she dropped?

While she was out of her clothes, however, she thought she might as well take a shower. And, having taken a shower, she looked at her nails which she thought could do with a tiny bit of attention before dinner that evening, and wrapped a housecoat around her prior to getting busy with emery board and nail buffer.

Quite what time it was when she yawned and decided to lie on top of her bed for a minute or two she had no idea. What she did have some idea about was that when she woke up it was dark outside. Swiftly she switched on some light, switched the light off again when she remembered about mosquitoes, then went to close the sliding door to the balcony. Only when she had the light on again did she go racing to pick up her watch.

Relief cascaded in as she saw that it was only seven o'clock. The few Egyptians she knew dined fairly late, so, although His Lordship next door had not given her any idea of what time she was to be ready, she didn't think he would come calling before eight. Just in case, though, she hadn't better hang about.

At twenty to eight, she had showered again, was dressed in her cream silk dress and had applied her make-up. A few minutes later she was re-checking that her long ash-blonde hair was all right when she heard what she thought was the door to the adjacent room opening and closing.

She knew her ears had not played her false when she heard someone walking by her door call a civilised greeting in passing, then heard Thane's voice reply, 'Good evening'.

Most oddly, then, her heart began to absurdly misbehave itself, but she had less than two seconds to pull herself together, because two seconds later there was a rap on her door. Joss took another second in which to look in her mirror again and in which to have a last-minute anxiety about the suitability of her dress after all. Then, going to the door, she remembered the document wallet she had walked away from Thane with and turned back to get it. Then she went and opened the door to him.

Then she forgot completely any nerves about whether her dress was suitable or not, because Thane, freshly shaven and in a dinner jacket, was something else again. Why her heart should suddenly start to race like an express train, as she looked at him, she didn't have time to analyse. But it did race, and she felt all at once too choked to speak as she saw his eyes go over her, starting at her shining hair and slightly flushed cheeks to skim over her breasts, waist and hips, and back up to her mouth, and finally his grey eyes pierced into her large brown eyes.

'W-will I do?' she enquired as coolly as her husky throat would allow.

'You look stunning—and you know it,' he told her sharply, which manner of compliment left her feeling a glow to hear him say she looked stunning, while at the same time she felt like boxing his ears that he should intimate that she had merely been fishing for compliments, or, worse, that she was conceited.

'Shall I bring this?' she queried coldly, holding up the document case as he stood back from her door.

'It would be rather pointless to come without it, wouldn't you say?' he drawled, and, leaving her room, Joss closed the door with a bang that resounded all the way up the corridor. Immediately she was sorry, but one of these days she was going to crown the swine!

Yazid Rashwan had sent a chauffeur-driven car to the hotel to pick them up, and, with Yazid's villa being some twenty minutes' drive away, Joss had time to get her rattled temper under control.

She still had the document case in her possession when a servant opened the door to the many-roomed, sumptuous home of the man who was the Osiris Corporation. Then Yazid Rashwan was there.

'My friend!' he greeted Thane warmly, and when the two had shaken hands, 'Miss Harding,' he easily remembered her name. 'Come and meet my wife.' And all three of them went to a graceful drawing-room where a charming and elegant woman of about fifty and who was dressed in a long black evening gown came forward.

'Welcome to my home,' she bade them both, though it was clear that she had met Thane before. Then suddenly Khalil Rashwan appeared.

'Josslyn!' he exclaimed as he came rushing forward to take both her hands in his. 'I have spent many long minutes in listening for the car to arrive—and then I missed it.'

'How are you, Khalil?' she asked him pleasantly, and might have asked him how he had found Japan, had his father not reminded him of his manners.

'You remember Thane, my son?' he enquired, and Khalil dropped her hands to go and shake hands with Thane.

'Please take a seat here, Miss Harding,' Yazid's wife smiled.

'Thank you,' Joss smiled back, and invited, 'Call me Joss, everybody does.'

'You never told me!' Khalil broke in as he quickly occupied the seat beside her on a luxurious couch.

'She doesn't tell everyone,' Thane commented drily.

Joss ignored him and was soon in conversation with Khalil's mother, who was soon inviting her to call her Noura, her first name. They spent quite some time in the pleasant drawing-room with conversation flowing easily, though with Thane, Joss observed, for all his outwardly urbane manner, giving her the occasional benefit of a steely look.

Seated as they were, no one else but Khalil, who was still right next to her, would have been able to witness Thane's cutting glances, but it didn't seem to bother Thane if Khalil saw or if he didn't. Not that Khalil seemed interested in looking anywhere but at her. Which, Joss knew full well, was what Thane's arctic glances were all about. Though from where she viewed it, short of insulting the whole family by suddenly coldly telling Khalil to go and sit somewhere else, she didn't see what she could do about it.

'How did you like Japan?' she got the question in when Khalil moved a few inches closer, and under cover of turning to address him she managed to move a few inches away.

'You were not there,' he said succinctly, and as Joss caught Thane's frown she started to hate Thane and began to wish she had never come.

She had some escape from Khalil's attentions when they went in to dinner. She was seated at the right hand of Yazid, and although Khalil was at the other side of her with Thane sitting to the right of Noura around the circular table, there was some space between them.

'Seif Ismail is here in Luxor,' Yazid mentioned to Thane during the main course of *lahma mahshiya*, which was beef stuffed with cheese and served with sundry salads. 'I've suggested that he might call later this evening.'

'I think that's an excellent idea,' Thane replied lightly, and Joss knew then that he had fully expected the Egyptian lawyer to put in an appearance before the contract was initialled, and that indeed he would have been surprised if he did not do so.

'Would you like more salad, Joss?' Khalil enquired attentively.

'Thank you, I've ample,' she told him, and later had the same treatment when, as she finished a delicious helping of a pressed apricot pudding which had mixed nuts and raisins in it, and went by the name of *mihallabiyet 'amar eldin*, he asked, 'Did you enjoy your pudding?'

'Very much,' she smiled.

'You would like some more?' he asked, and as Joss politely told him that, delicious though it was, she had had sufficient, she understood why it was that she could not take him seriously, or take seriously Thane's belief that Khalil was panting to get her into bed. For older than her Khalil might be, but he seemed so young. Thane now, with his sophistication... Abruptly her thoughts ceased. Grief—what had Thane got to do with anything!

They had returned to the drawing-room and were drinking coffee when it was brought home to Joss that Thane Addison had a great deal to do with *everything*. She realised that, possibly because they were the only two English people in this Egyptian household, she was being over-sensitive where Thane was concerned, but she was most definitely feeling vibes of animosity coming from him. While he and Yazid were getting along like a house on fire, all she was getting from Thane was a tight-lipped expression because she was again seated on the settee with Khalil.

Which, since it had been Khalil who had manoeuvred himself into a position next to her while his mother had been instructing the servants about something, was none of her making. In actual fact, she was starting to find Khalil just a wee bit tedious. She could not remember him being so—'cloying' seemed about the best word to fit, before he had gone to Japan, so had he changed, or had she?

Whatever the truth of the matter, she was starting to feel quite exhausted from the effort of fending off his attentions while at the same time, for fear of offending his parents who clearly loved and indulged him, maintaining a friendliness with him. She would not have minded at all had Thane suddenly declared that they must return to their hotel—indeed, she was more than ready to go—but she knew she was not going anywhere until *he* said so.

She grew hopeful that they would soon be able to leave, however, when a few moments later a manservant entered the room and said a few discreet words in Arabic which meant nothing to her, but which, having overheard Thane speaking the language on the phone a time or two, she knew he would understand.

It was out of courtesy to her, she realised, that Yazid said in English, 'Seif Ismail is waiting in my study—shall we adjourn, Thane?'

'Of course,' Thane said easily, and with a look over to where Joss sat he was on his feet. For one lovely moment she thought his look meant that she was to go into the study with them. But that hope died a death when, observing her slight movement as if she was about to rise, he stopped her by the quiet question, 'Have you got the contracts, Joss?'

She smiled at him, and as she bent down to the side of the settee where she had left the document case prior to going in to dinner, she wished she hadn't smiled. He'd only called her Joss so that the others wouldn't know that she wasn't exactly flavour of the month where he was concerned that evening.

Taking up the leather wallet, she was about to unzip it to remove the documents he needed, when he stretched out a hand and took the wallet from her. Then, with a courteous 'Excuse me, Noura,' to his hostess, he went with Yazid Rashwan from the room.

Although Yazid's wife could not have been more charming, the next hour dragged by for Joss. Had it been just she and Noura there, there would have been no problem. But, with Khalil wanting to monopolise her, Joss was very hard put to it not to be sharp with him. Which, she realised, made him think—since she wasn't verbally slapping him down—that she was encouraging him.

'You've been to England, I expect?' she smiled at Noura when a discreet glance at the watch on Khalil's wrist showed that the three men had been in the study for over an hour.

'Many times,' Noura replied, and they spoke for some minutes about the various parts of Great Britain that Noura had visited, until Khalil, having had enough of being ignored, even briefly, decided to chime in.

'Perhaps you will show me around England the next time I make the trip?' he interrupted to suggest. 'Though first,' he said eagerly, 'you must allow me to show you my country.'

'There's—so much to see,' Joss was replying tactfully when, as his mother smiled indulgently, he caught hold of both her hands.

Several things happened at the same time then. With relief Joss heard sounds that told her that the business in the study was over. Then, as Khalil continued to keep tight hold of her hands and started to declare, 'You *must* allow me to show you, Joss. I will call...' all at once Thane was standing over them, and suddenly he was forcing Khalil to let go her hands by the simple expedient of pushing her document wallet at her.

Deciding that it might be politic to keep something in her hands, Joss hung on to the wallet as she took a swift glance at Yazid's face. He seemed well pleased, she saw, and, transferring her glance to Thane, she observed that he seemed equally well pleased. Sensing, though, that she was in his black books, she knew better than to meet his eyes.

'If my religion did not forbid alcohol, we would celebrate with champagne,' Yazid confirmed that all had gone well as he grinned to Thane. 'But, since champagne is out of the question, may I offer you some other refreshment?'

Tactfully Thane turned down the offer, then suggested that it was time that they returned to their hotel. It was another half an hour before Yazid allowed them to go and they shook hands all round, and another ten minutes, with Khalil coming out and seeing Joss into the car, before the chauffeur headed back to the hotel.

Joss's feelings were a mixture of relief to be away from Khalil, and a mixture of being exceedingly upset with Thane that, when she wanted to congratulate him most sincerely for all he had achieved, by his very uncommunicative attitude he had made it impossible for her to voice those congratulations.

She left him talking to the chauffeur when they reached their hotel, and went swiftly to reception. 'Can I have my room key, please?' she asked the receptionist, giving her room number. Then, because it seemed petty not to do so, she asked for Thane's key too.

He was heading towards the desk as she turned round. Without a word she held out his key and stood bravely still while his grim glance flicked over her and the picture she made in her dress.

I wonder if he still thinks I look stunning, she thought sourly as he raised a hand and, without a word, took the key from her. It seemed that not only did he never say 'please', but that he had added 'thank you' to his list of words never to leave his lips.

Why that should bother her, she didn't know, but suddenly, and to her horror, she discovered that she was feeling quite weepy. 'Goodnight!' she said quickly, and went swiftly towards the lifts.

He had not answered her goodnight, nor had he followed her to where the lifts were. And that was all right by her, she thought, still having to swallow hard. She got into the lift and stabbed the number six button, and was sure she didn't care a light.

She was leaving the lift, however, when with a shock that threatened to make her knees buckle she realised that she did care! She cared very much. Suddenly—while starting to fume that she didn't know what was the matter with the wretched man that he should be so grim-faced when, after what he had achieved, he should be dancing a jig that his work was good as over—she halted.

All at once her heart gave a mighty lurch. And she knew then, with overwhelming clarity, that she didn't want it to be over! Then, like a bolt from the blue, she knew exactly what was the matter with *her*. She was in love with him! Oh, dear heaven, what utter madness!

CHAPTER SEVEN

SUNDAY dawned with Joss wide awake in her bed and knowing that she had done the unthinkable. She had done what Thane had more or less warned her not to do at their very first meeting—she had fallen in love with him.

Leaving her bed, she showered and dressed in light cotton trousers of pale lemon and topped them with a lemon T-shirt. Then, for something to do, she made her bed and tidied her room and, in need of escape from the four walls, though being careful not to make the smallest sound that would echo up the corridors and disturb other residents, she left her room.

She was not feeling in the slightest hungry, but was glad that the hotel's restaurant opened very early to serve breakfast. 'Good morning, madam,' a smiling waiter greeted her as she went into the restaurant.

'Good morning,' she replied, and went and helped herself from the self-service stand to a glass of *karkade*, a pleasant fruit-tasting drink made from dried hibiscus petals.

There was ample space in the restaurant, and Joss sat down at the nearest table and reflected that things looked no better from down here than up in her room.

'Coffee, madam?' the waiter who had greeted her approached her with a coffee-pot.

'Thank you,' she accepted, but the coffee went cold as she sipped her *karkade* and thought of Thane Addison and of what a total idiot she had been to fall in love with him. It had been coming on for some time—only now, now that she knew, was she able to realise that all the signs had been there, but she had been too blind to see.

Well, much good would being in love with Thane do her, she sighed. She had the example of Paula Ingram before her to realise that she stood as much chance of Thane reciprocating her feelings as of the Nile freezing over. Unlike Paula Ingram, though, Joss knew she would die rather than let Thane know how she felt about him.

Starting to feel a little agitated lest she had given away any hint that she was starting to care for him, Joss went through agonies, and owned that she was more than a little fed up.

In desperation she turned her thoughts from Thane, but only grew more fed up when thoughts of Khalil Rashwan entered her head. Somehow she just didn't feel like coping with Khalil today, yet she thought she wouldn't need any prizes for guessing that he was likely to be on the telephone more or less as soon as she got back to her room.

That was—if she was in her room! Suddenly, from being totally fed up, Joss suddenly started to rebel. Why should she stay in her room? It was Sunday, for goodness' sake!

In the next few minutes she had left the restaurant and was taking the lift upwards. She had no idea what Thane's plans were for her that day, but he had intimated at the outset that they would be in Luxor for a few days, so he couldn't mean them to fly back to Alexandria that day. But with the job she was there to do virtually completed as far as she could tell, she just couldn't see any good reason why she should stay around the hotel.

Getting out of the lift on the sixth floor, Joss went quickly and quietly along the corridor. As she went by

Thane's room, however, the feeling of wanting to see him became so intense that she almost knocked on his door. She was then absolutely appalled that her feelings for him should so dent her pride, and she went swiftly past his door to insert her key into the next-door room and hurriedly shut herself in.

Only when that mad moment of impetuosity had passed did she realise the strength of her emotion for him. How could she have gone to him—what if he'd glimpsed from anything in her expression how she felt about him?

The realisation that any such knowledge he might receive would for certain see him dismissing her on the spot gave Joss the stiffening she needed. Ten seconds later she had herself firmly under control as she picked up the phone and asked to be put through to his room. She checked her watch; it had just gone seven-thirty. Sunday or no Sunday, she saw no reason why Thane, the cause of her sleeplessness, should sleep on undisturbed.

'Aeywae,' answered a voice she would know anywhere, although he spoke in Arabic. That voice, alert and awake, let her know that he had probably been up and about for ages.

Her knees went weak. She sank down to sit on the bed, and gripping hard on to the phone as if her life depended upon it, she announced herself coolly, 'It's Josslyn Harding. I wondered what plans you have for today?'

Silence was her answer for a few moments, then, 'Why?' he questioned bluntly, and, loving him, at the same time she hated his aggression.

She took a long and steadying breath, then replied as evenly as she could, 'Because, if we're not going back to Alexandria today, and if you've no need of me, then I wouldn't mind the day off.'

She had spoken calmly and politely. His reply was harsh and rapid. 'What for?' he demanded, and one of the sudden bursts of temper which she had become subject to since knowing him immediately flared up again.

'Because I've been in Egypt four weeks tomorrow and I've seen nothing yet but airports and offices,' she retorted hotly, stretching the truth a little in her anger.

His reply was swift and harsh. 'Do as much sight-seeing as you want—I've no need of you!' he hurled at her. With that his phone went down, and Joss's breath caught in her throat.

She tried to rally herself by remembering that he jolly well needed her secretarial skills, didn't he? But she knew she was only fooling herself. With or without her speedy and proficient-plus ability at the typewriter, he had no need of her. Any secretary would suit. Look at how easily Paula Ingram had been replaced.

Damn him, she refused to be downcast, and was about to charge indignantly from her room when suddenly her leather document wallet caught her eye. Heavens! she gulped, as she recalled how she had left the wallet and all the highly confidential matter it contained lying about when she'd gone down to the restaurant.

She went over to it, picked it up and had a silent battle on the subject of going and knocking at the next-door room, and handing the wallet over to Thane. Against that, though, why should she? He'd pushed it at her last night, hadn't he?

The matter was resolved when just then she heard the clear sound of him leaving his room and securing his door. For one panicky moment she thought he was coming to see her, and her heart started to race. Her heartbeats steadied down again, though, when she heard his footsteps moving away in the opposite direction.

Well, she jolly well wasn't going to wait around for him to come back from his breakfast, she decided, pride arriving to give her aggression a much-needed boost. Though before she went anywhere, pride or no pride, her efficient secretarial self surfaced. Unzipping the wallet, she checked its contents. She anticipated that there would be only one copy of the contract inside, and indeed would have been most surprised had the two copies she had originally put there still been there. But everything was as she expected, she saw with a touch of relief—her notes, her shorthand pad and one copy of the contract, now initialled by both Thane and Yazid.

Zipping up the wallet once more, Joss knew she would not leave it lying about now that she had remembered it. When she thought about it, she realised that it made no difference which of them had the wallet, she or Thane, for his room was a replica of hers, so she might as well hide the folder in her room as wait around for him to come back and take it to him. Besides, she wasn't feeling very friendly towards him just now.

Five minutes later she left her room and walked to the lift, knowing that the wallet which she had wrapped in the dress which she had worn last night, and which she had then put inside her suitcase and locked, was as safe as it was going to be.

She descended in the lift wondering if the responsibility of looking after that confidential document which both Thane and Yazid now considered binding had not made her a little paranoid. It was for sure that Thane had no such concern since he was probably, at this very moment, tucking in to a hearty breakfast.

With that thought, she stepped out of the lift, walked about five yards into the vast lobby, then had all the evidence she needed that if Thane had breakfasted, he had made short work of his breakfast. Because, tall, broad-shouldered and straight, he was now standing at the reception desk making some enquiry.

Feeling instantly fluttery inside, Joss had about a second in which to decide whether she was ready to pass the time of day with him in person or if she wasn't. She had intended handing her room key in, but he was standing more or less in the exact spot that she had been making for.

She hesitated, and halted, and it was at that moment that Thane finished his enquiry and turned and spotted her. Feeling frozen, Joss tried to compose her features as, casually, Thane strolled over to her.

What she had expected him to say she had no idea, but after the way he had not so long ago snarled at her, his tone was very much different from the tone she had expected. For, looking down into her face, he asked pleasantly, 'Off to take in the sights?'

'Yes,' she replied, and, with her heart pounding erratically just at the sight of him, she knew she should walk on her way—and yet she seemed powerless to do so.

'Where are you going to start?' Thane, instead of moving on as she fully expected, stayed to enquire.

'I'm—not sure yet,' she replied, her heartbeats racing into overdrive when suddenly he smiled down at her.

'Then maybe I'd better come with you,' he commented, and while not believing her hearing Joss just stood and stared up at him, 'That is,' he began, and she could hear definite chinks of ice entering his voice, 'unless you've arranged other company?'

Wordlessly, she shook her head, and when Thane suddenly smiled again there was no way she could prevent the smile that started somewhere deep inside her from coming out into the open.

'What are we waiting for?' he queried, and before she had in any way collected her breath he had taken her room key from her, deposited it at the desk and turned back to take hold of her arm. Then he was escorting her outside to where several taxis were awaiting customers.

Joss was still finding it difficult to believe that what was happening was actually happening, when she sat in a taxi beside Thane, heading for the Valley of the Kings.

Minutes later she had recovered a little to decide that, since it seemed that the gods had decreed she should have some small time with him, she would snatch at it with both hands. There was no way in which she was going to turn her back on this unexpected bonus. She was going to enjoy every moment of this time of Thane not barking at her, or being generally aggressive. She had a few happy memories of him. Simply—she wanted more.

'The place seems crowded already!' she exclaimed when some while later their taxi-driver pulled up in a car park.

'Word must have got around that in a little while the sun will be unbearable,' Thane replied, and as Joss realised that everyone seemed to have the same idea of getting to the towering sun-scorched hills early before the sun turned everyone into grease spots, he gave the driver a few instructions in Arabic and escorted her away from the taxi.

Joss had no idea if Thane had asked the driver to wait, or what he had told him. But how they got back was, just then, immaterial to her. She was here, in the Valley of the Kings with Thane Addison, the man she loved, and nothing else mattered.

She was happier than she could ever remember as together they first walked through an area where souvenir sellers were pressing anyone who caught their eyes to buy.

'For you, madam,' one man in a green galabiyah and wearing a white headdress implored, holding up a T-shirt.

'No, thank you,' she replied, not firmly enough, she realised.

'But yes, madam,' he insisted, and would have hung it over her arm had not Thane spoke a little sharply to him in Arabic.

She knew better the next time when a similarly dressed trader tried to press a green marble scarab into her hands. Quickly she thrust her hands into her pockets. Then, looking at Thane, she heard him laugh. It was a memory to store forever.

They did buy something before they had run the full gauntlet of the souvenir sellers, though. At least Thane did. 'Just a moment,' he murmured, and taking Joss by the arm he guided her over to where one cheerfully smiling Egyptian was selling hats. 'This one, I think,' he said, taking up a white cotton one. And before Joss knew what he was about, he had gone through the good-humoured game of bargaining for it, and had then paid for it and was turning to place it on her head.

Instinctively her hands went up to adjust it. 'Does it look all right?' she asked, and found she was having difficulty in breathing as, having invited his inspection, she found herself looking up into a pair of serious grey eyes.

'You've been told you're beautiful, of course,' he commented, his expression unsmiling.

But, while she was thrilled that Thane thought her beautiful, she didn't want him serious, not now, not at this time of her storing up happy memories. For 'serious' was only a few steps away from 'aggression', she felt. So she replied, 'Of course,' and grinned cheekily up at him. For a second or two he continued to survey her solemnly. Then suddenly, to her immense delight, he grinned in return, and Joss's cup of happiness was full.

It was an upward climb to the tombs of the kings, but no one was hurrying. Roads had been made in the rocky sun-drenched hillside where not one blade of grass grew as far as Joss could see.

The hills were impressive, as too were the tombs that had been hewn out of the rock. 'Have you been here before?' she asked Thane as they stood in a small queue waiting to descend into the tomb of Rameses the Sixth.

'It's always worth a second or third visit,' he replied pleasantly, and indeed, Joss was spellbound when their turn came to descend the deep stairway, and to see the splendid wall drawings of over three thousand years ago.

They had to queue a second time when, having climbed up from what were the depths, they moved to the smallest tomb, that of Tutankhamun. There were excellent frescoes to be seen, and, while most of the artefacts had been transferred to the Egyptian Museum in Cairo, the golden sarcophagus that had held the mummified body of the young king was absolutely breathtaking in its splendour.

Joss blinked against the bright sunlight when she and Thane came out from the tomb, and she had no demur to make when he told her, 'Put your sunglasses on.' For once she was rather enjoying being bossed about by him.

With the day hotting up uncomfortably, however, they did not stay in the Valley of the Kings for much longer than to take in a couple of lesser known tombs and to generally absorb the atmosphere. Then Thane, with a glance at her fair skin, was suggesting that they returned the way they had come.

'We'll stop and quench our thirst somewhere less crowded,' he mooted, eyeing the large refreshment building where the world and all comers were milling about.

'Fine,' Joss replied, her heart lifting. Her time, this time, this special precious time with him, wasn't over yet, then!

The taxi-driver *was* waiting and, spotting them straight away, he immediately left a group of other drivers he had been happily chatting with and came hurrying back to his taxi.

Maybe it was because her discovery that she was in love with Thane had made her time with him so precious, but it seemed that time was going fast when, in next to no time, she was seated with him in the cool garden room of a hotel. She had half drunk the glass of lemonade in front of her, while Thane had all but finished his.

To her delight, however, he seemed in no hurry to escort her back to their hotel, but appeared to have all the time in the world as they discussed any topic that occurred to them. By unspoken mutual consent, it seemed, not once did either of them mention work. Though when she was positively itching to know more about him, it was Joss who was on the answering end of the questioning. 'Do you live at home with your parents?' he enquired idly on one occasion.

She shook her head and, taking another sip of her lemonade, revealed, 'My parents live in Eastbourne. I left home some years ago.'

'You have a flat?'

'A small one, but mine own,' she smiled, and took another drink of her lemonade when she observed that his glass was empty. 'At least, I'm buying it courtesy of a mortgage,' she added, and wanted quite desperately to ask him about his parents and if he had a flat, a house, or whatever. But suddenly nerves—which prior to her knowledge that she loved him had been non-existent—were starting to bite. What if he thought she was deliberately prolonging drinking her lemonade just to keep him in conversation? On that pride-threatening thought, Joss finished the rest of her lemonade.

Then, like music in her ears, she heard Thane enquire pleasantly, 'Where to now?'

'Um...' she hesitated, wondering if she should take up more of his time. But she loved him, and suddenly she could no more turn down what the gods were offering than fly. Perhaps she was being greedy, but she had been in Thane's company, his pleasant company, for a couple of hours now—and she wanted more. So she told him, 'I haven't been to a bazaar yet,' adding quickly, 'A proper one, I mean—not the touristy one.'

'I know exactly what you mean,' he smiled, and to prove it a taxi was soon dropping them off in a market place where she could see no sign of any other European.

Like a miser Joss stored up memory after memory, of galabiyah-robed men, and of women clothed from head to foot all in black. Of stalls of oranges and green bananas. Of dusty, sandy streets, of rush-woven baskets.

There were more attractive sights than the fly-smothered meat laid bare on an open-air butcher's table, but it all added up to an entirely fantastic atmosphere as far as she was concerned. The most gigantic cabbages she had ever seen were for sale from one trader, while opposite him a young man was selling a whole range of aromatic spices.

Then, to crown what was for her the most wonderful of experiences, they came to a part of the market where on the outside of a small building, and hanging high in the air, were rugs of many different hues and sizes.

'That one is just crying out to go home to my dining-room,' Joss told Thane a trace regretfully, and before she knew what was happening, he had put his hand on her elbow and was guiding her inside. And, all before she had time to observe that there were shelves and shelves of silks and cottons, a couple of stools had been conjured up out of somewhere, both she and Thane had a glass of tea in their hands, and the rug she had admired was laid out on the floor for their inspection.

The rug was larger than she had at first thought, but that was a point in its favour from her point of view. Though she had to own to a feeling of being swept along by the trader's enthusiasm, and she was glad of Thane's calming presence when, looking down at her, he enquired, 'Is it still crying out to go to your home?'

'It's beautiful!' she breathed, and raised gentle brown velvety eyes to his. For a second then, as without a word Thane stared into her eyes, she thought she felt a sudden tension in the air. Then nerves got to her, nerves that he might see her caring for him in her eyes, and swiftly she turned her attention back to the carpet. 'Truly beautiful,' she added, 'but I can't possibly buy it.'

Long moments of silence followed, and she thought Thane was not going to make any comment. But, just as she thought they would thank the carpet-seller for his tea, and leave, Thane remarked, 'I think you could get it for as little as sixty English pounds.'

'Honestly?' she exclaimed, and, her appetite well and truly whetted, 'But how will I get it home?' she queried, unable to see herself rolling it up and carrying it over her shoulder, no matter how hard she tried.

'Leave it to me—I'll show you a trick,' he teased, and she loved him, and after much haggling which embarrassed her slightly but which the carpet-seller, his assistants and in fact everyone else seemed to take thorough delight in, she bought the rug which it had never been her intention to buy when she had left her bed that morning. Then Thane was taking her in a taxi to air-freight it back to England. She was still in a state of euphoria when he suggested lunch.

She was sitting across the table from him, however, when she realised why it was that he was being so kind to her that day. With the initialling of that contract, he was released from the stresses of his business problems for a while. Today he could relax and make the most of a well-earned break.

Which thought made her sensitive to him and made her want him to enjoy the day as much as she was enjoying it. So she put any reserves of shyness and pride aside, and chatted in friendly fashion throughout lunch, and discovered, without quite knowing how the subject had come up, that she was telling him about her hankering to see the Pyramids.

'You haven't seen the Pyramids yet?' he enquired, in some small surprise.

'I've been to Cairo twice,' she informed him, and just had to smile as she added, 'My boss is a bit of a slave-driver and . . .'

'Say no more,' he cut in, his eyes on the sweet curve of her mouth. 'If you'll permit me, I'll have words with him and see if we can't arrange for you to visit the Pyramids one day soon.' Joss saw the light of laughter dancing in his eyes, and fell deeper in love with him than ever.

When she had finished her meal and had begun to think that her day with him was over, however, she could hardly believe her good fortune that it seemed it was not!

'Have you had enough?' Thane enquired, and she was unsure if he meant to eat, or of sightseeing.

'You've been very kind,' she replied quietly.

'Which means that you'd like to see more, but that you're afraid of encroaching on my time?' Thane guessed, giving her a heart-fluttering amicable look.

'Something like that,' she murmured, and absolutely adored him when he replied,

'After the way I've worked you, I think that to put myself at your disposal for the whole of today is the least I can do.'

They were on their way to see the Temple of Karnak, with Joss being of the opinion that of the two of them he had certainly worked the harder, when she wondered if he had grown to like her. He must like her, mustn't he? Or was it just a case of two English people who knew each other and, with nothing else pressing, were simply passing a day in each other's company?

At that point Joss realised how ready she was to gather up any crumb of a suggestion that Thane liked her. But, since he was never likely to tell her—and probably never gave such matters a moment's thought—she would be content with what she had and to do all she could to ensure that nothing should spoil this most wonderful of days.

That the Temple of Karnak was impressive was, she thought, an understatement. The place was alive with tourists, and as Joss walked with Thane through a corridor where ram-headed sphinx-like statues flanked either side of the walkway, she was once more in awe. There was much to see, for the complex of the temple was, as well as being magnificent, enormous. It housed the Hypostyle Hall, which was reputed to be the largest hall of any temple in the world. At one time it had been the religious centre of Thebes and a place where for two thousand years the Pharaohs had built their monuments.

All in all there was much too much for Joss to absorb in one visit, and she knew she would be foolish to try. So she settled for being content just to be there—and with Thane.

'You'll be exhausted if we carry on at this rate,' he teased as they came away from the temple, and while she thrilled to his teasing, she was positively overjoyed when he suggested, 'How about returning to our hotel for an hour or two, then coming back here for the Son et Lumière tonight? We could fit in dinner afterwards.'

Joss tried desperately hard not to instantly grab at his suggestion. 'That sounds very nice,' she accepted pleasantly, and was further delighted when he hired a horse-drawn calèche to take them back to the hotel, then—and she knew she was fooling herself, but by then she didn't care—just as if he couldn't bear to be parted from her, Thane proposed that they shared a pot of tea in one of the lounges before they went up to their rooms.

By that lovely time, it was already dusk. 'See you in an hour,' Thane said as they parted, and Joss went into her room and closed the door, unable to believe that, incredibly, she had spent a whole day with Thane with not one cross or harsh word passing between them.

She had a quick shower and wondered if it was because of her new-found love for him that she was not flaring up at the least little pinprick. Or was it on account of the fact that Thane had not delivered any barbed comments that day? Whatever it was, it was marvellous to have Thane in this relaxed and charming mood. She had never felt happier.

A slight dent was to appear in her feeling of happiness a short while later, however. She had changed into fresh trousers and opted to wear a lightweight sweater. She then decided that, since Thane had said they would have dinner after the Son et Lumière, an embroidered cotton shirt would be more appropriate. Time was running short when she exchanged the sweater for a shirt, and she was just in the middle of recombing her hair when for no particular reason she turned her head in the direction of the door, and for the first time noticed what she had been too much involved with her thoughts to notice before. Someone, at some time, had slipped a note under her door.

Swiftly she went and picked it up and opened out the missive to find it was from Khalil. Her spirits dipped as she read that he had been trying and trying to get in touch with her that day. Had she not realised that he would do so? he asked. Would she please telephone him the moment she received his letter? He would wait by the telephone until then.

Slowly Joss wandered over to the telephone. She did not want to ring Khalil, she admitted. But then neither did she want him to spend any more time waiting by the phone. Not that she truly believed that he was doing anything of the sort. But... Her thoughts suddenly ceased when just then she heard the sound of Thane leaving his room. In a flash she was over at her dressing-table, slipping Khalil's note into a drawer while at the same time she took up the comb and hastily tidied up her hair.

Then the buzzer at the side of her door sounded, and she went to answer it. Thane had changed too, and her heart beat crazily at just the sight of him as he looked into her face for several long moments. Then a lazy kind of smile crossed his features, a smile she found attractive and heartwarming, as he remarked, 'You'll need a jacket.'

'Won't be a moment,' she told him, and dipped back into her room to take a lightweight windcheater out of her wardrobe.

Thane had not spoken falsely about her need of a jacket, Joss discovered, for by the time they returned to the Temple of Karnak, something of a sandstorm was blowing up. She was most glad of her windcheater when the Son et Lumière proved to be unlike any sound and light show she had been to before in that they did not at first take seats to sit and watch. At first they stood, with hundreds of other like-minded patrons, held back by a rope until the rope was lowered and they were allowed to move forward through the area where the ram-headed sphinxes she had seen that afternoon still stood guard. They walked some way through tall majestic pillars on which were engraved in deep relief the tales of gods and kings. They then came to another roped-off area, and clear female and then male voices intoned over loudspeakers the story of ancient Thebes while lights played on walls and monuments.

Joss was totally entranced as that rope too was lowered and Thane took hold of her arm lest, in the crush of people surging forward, they got separated.

A swirl of wind caused her hair to fly and she closed her eyes as a shower of sand made straight for her. 'Have you got your hat with you?' Thane bent down to ask.

'My sun-hat?'

'This is no time for vanity,' he said, and in the darkness she was sure that he was smiling.

She smiled too, realising as she put her hand into her shoulder-bag that at one time she might have reared up at his remark—missing his humour entirely. A second later she was taking the hat he had bought her out of her bag and pulling it down on her head.

In all, she thought they walked around for about an hour, and although by then she felt decidedly gritty from the sand and in the most definite need of a bath, she would not have missed the experience for anything.

Though she full well knew that a good deal of her pleasure stemmed from the fact that she was there with Thane.

He must be enjoying it too, she felt, because although he must be suffering too from the gritty effects of the sandstorm, he had made no suggestion to abandon the show, as a few people around them had.

The finale of Son et Lumière took place at the Sacred Lake, and it was here, facing the lake, that row upon row of seats had been installed. Joss spent the most blissful half-hour just seated next to Thane. The commentary passed her by as she gave herself up to the pure enjoyment of sitting next to him in the dark, where he was not likely to see the truth in her eyes, and of loving him.

'Enjoy that?' he enquired, once the performance was over and they, along with those that remained, made their way along the rows of seats to the exits.

'Wouldn't have missed it for anything,' she told him truthfully. 'How about you?'

'What's a bit of sand between friends?' he replied, and she thought, Oh, Thane, I do so love you!

'What indeed?' she laughed, totally enchanted by him—he had suggested that they were friends.

'I don't know about you, but I could do with a shower before we eat,' he said a minute or so later when, with everyone scrambling for taxis, the taxi they had arrived in drew up beside them.

Inwardly, Joss was laughing. Trust him to have transport organised, she thought, as they got into the taxi. 'That's one of the best suggestions I've heard all day,' she smiled, and leaned back contentedly. Unbelievably, her day with Thane was not yet over. Once they had returned to the hotel and washed the sand away, they would meet again for a meal.

'How long?' she questioned when at the doors of their rooms they were about to separate. 'Half an hour?' she suggested.

'You've a head start on most other women.' Thane looked back at her. 'Make it twenty minutes.'

Joss was still inwardly laughing when, inside her room, she hurriedly brushed the sand from her hair, then stripped off and got into the shower. Oh, how she loved him! There would be no time to wash her hair, she mused happily, but who cared, she'd put up with that for the chance of seeing Thane again so soon.

She was just stepping out of the shower, though, when, making her realise that she had spent longer than she had intended over her ablutions, she heard her door buzzer sound.

Blotting most of the moisture from her skin, she tossed the towel back into the bathroom and quickly reached for her housecoat. Head start on most other women or no, she was just going to have to beg Thane for those ten extra minutes.

'I'm not . . .' she began as she pulled back the door, but her voice tailed off, for it was not Thane who stood there, but Khalil Rashwan. A Khalil Rashwan who was looking most upset. Suddenly Joss sensed trouble. 'Khalil . . .' she said his name in some instinctive move to ward off what—she wasn't sure.

'Why did you not telephone me?' he asked her angrily.

'I—er—haven't had time,' she replied honestly, if, she realised later, not very tactfully.

'You had my letter, but you didn't have time . . .' Khalil choked, his face working. 'Did I not tell you that I would wait?'

'Yes, but——' she tried to get in to calm him down, but could see when he took a step nearer to her that she had made things worse, not better.

'I've waited all this day for you to call me!' he ranted as she quickly took a step back. Then as he took another step forward and she backed again, she discovered that they were both in her room and that Khalil was going completely out of control. 'Don't you know what is in my heart for you?' he cried, and before she could stop him he had made a sudden lunge for her and made a desperate attempt to kiss her.

Panicking wildly, Joss equally desperately tried to make sure that he did not kiss her. There were only one man's lips she wanted—anyone else's would be offensive. Saving her breath to help with her energy, she pushed with all her might to break the suffocating embrace of the arms he had about her. Then suddenly, through her panic, she heard a mighty roar—and it did not come from Khalil. For Thane was all at once there, and in no time she was free.

Not that Khalil let her go voluntarily, but when Thane caught hold of him, he had no other choice. She had thought Thane might be physically powerful. He proved it. As if Khalil weighed nothing, he plucked him away from her. Then, after letting fly with a stream of Arabic directed at Khalil, Thane let fly with his fist and sent him sprawling. Khalil was still sitting in a stunned heap, when with more unfriendly-sounding Arabic Thane went over and threw him out of the room.

Having looked on with horrified eyes, Joss didn't know what to do first, go and see if Khalil was all right, or thank Thane for coming in when he had.

The decision about what to do, however, was resolved when Thane slammed the door on Khalil and turned back to her. But when Joss opened her mouth to thank him, she was shaken to see that he looked in no mood to want her thanks. Just one glance at his enraged expression was enough to tell her that if he was furious with Khalil Rashwan, then he was doubly furious with her, and she somehow got the impression that she'd be better off not saying anything at all!

CHAPTER EIGHT

WORDLESSLY Joss stared at Thane's hostile and un-friendly expression, and her spirits sank lower than ever. How she had ever thought or hoped never to see him hostile with her again, she couldn't think, because, as if they had not exchanged one pleasant word with each other all that wonderful day, he was now looking at her with positive chips of dislike in his eyes.

'I warned you!' he rounded on her, his grating tone all the confirmation she needed that the wonder of the day had been one-sided only—dear heaven, had she been in a fool's paradise! 'I told you he was panting to get you into bed,' he snarled, enraged, 'yet you still had to encourage him!'

'I didn't encourage him!' Joss erupted; she might be hurting inside, but she was nobody's doormat. 'All I ...'

'Of course you encouraged him!' barked Thane, his hands clenching and unclenching down by his side. 'Just as you encourage every man who comes within your orbit! You ...'

'That's most unfair!' she flew in explosively. 'I ...'

'Is it?' he rapped. 'Like hell it is! You've been giving me the green light all day, for one!' he told her thunder-ously, and as Joss gasped and just had to defend herself against that—even if she lied herself silly—he came up close to her, his jaw jutting at a furious angle.

'I've done nothing of the sort!' she retorted. She had backed away from Khalil, but she stood her ground as she told Thane heatedly, 'If you've imagined for a moment that I've been giving you so much as a pale green light, then do you have one heck of an imagination!'

'Imagined it, did I?' he bellowed, and, clearly needled by her refusal to back down, 'We'll see, shall we!' he roared, and the next Joss knew was that he had hauled her into his arms and that his mouth was over hers.

'No!' She tried to push him away when she had the breath, but Thane was stronger than she, and furious into the bargain.

'Oh, but yes,' he grated, and claimed her lips again, pulling her housecoat-clad figure closer and yet closer to him, seeming to become the more enraged the more she struggled. 'Keep that up, sweetheart,' he told her harshly when next she managed to get her mouth free, 'and I shan't need any more encouragement!'

Abruptly, as the realisation flooded in that, instead of making Thane see that she didn't want his harsh kisses, she was only inflaming him to desire instead, Joss ceased struggling in his arms.

Thane kissed her again and, as he realised that she was no longer fighting him, some of the anger went from his kiss. Joss felt his kiss gentle out, and suddenly she found it impossible to just stand passive in his arms. She became vibrantly aware of him, of the freshly showered smell of him, and as all at once he pulled her that bit closer to him, suddenly she was leaning against him.

Time stood still for her as Thane kissed her and trailed kisses down her throat. In his arms was where she wanted to be—nothing else mattered. Her arms went up and around him, and her fingers went to his hair, still damp from the shower. 'Oh, Thane,' she breathed, and revelled in the feeling of closeness with him when he moved with her to lie down on the top of her bed.

Again and again he kissed her, and as a fire sprang to urgent life within her Joss responded ardently to his every kiss. When he pressed himself to her, she responded by pressing herself against him.

Desire for him spiralled in her so that she almost cried out his name again. Then some faint memory stirred that she was naked under her housecoat when Thane slipped his hand inside the front opening.

She clutched him desperately when his fingers unerringly came to circle her left breast, but she had no objection to make when he parted the folds of her gown and gazed down at the hardened pink peaks of her swollen breasts.

When he bent his head to kiss each breast in turn, Joss, with shaky fingers, undid the buttons on his shirt. A sigh of pure satisfaction left her when, after a few minutes of tenderly stroking and caressing her, Thane lowered his hair-roughened naked chest over the top of her uncovered silken breasts.

'Oh!' she sighed, in rapture at feeling his skin against her skin, his warmth against her warmth. Then Thane was kissing her again, and suddenly she was in a mindless vortex of wanting. Nothing mattered but Thane and that they shared of themselves in the most intimate way that there was.

She wanted to tell him there and then, I'm yours, but shyness suddenly attacked from nowhere and, when she had thought she no longer had any inhibitions, she was all at once too shy to tell him anything of what she was feeling.

Those unforeseen inhibitions were to trip her up yet again a moment later when Thane, after unbuttoning her housecoat the rest of the way, began to lay aside the folds and moved his head as if about to feast his eyes on the rest of her uncovered body.

'I...' she gasped chokily, and instinctively made to pull the folds of her housecoat close to again. A moment after that, she had recovered from her shyness, and was ready to make a small apology for being so self-conscious—now of all times.

But her apology never made it. For suddenly Thane had stilled, and as she looked up into his face, as he stared down at her pinkened skin and into her large melting eyes, it was as though he had suddenly come to to remember how furious he had been with her.

Then, to her utter bewilderment, he had rapidly jerked away from her and, having left the bed, his fury had returned when, glancing back to her, he snarled, 'Do your buttons up!'

More in haste than dignity, Joss sat up and somehow managed to expose more of her full breasts. With trembling hands she hastily pulled the edges of her robe together.

'W-what did I do?' she asked, still in a no-man's-land, and sorely needing some guidance.

'Do?' he charged. 'Plenty!' And while she just sat there and stared in stupefied amazement, he turned before her very eyes into the man she had once hated but had thought, in her naïveté, that she would never see again. 'Thanks to you and your wanton behaviour you've ruined what has taken me months to achieve!' he berated her arctically.

'I...!' she gasped, and could hardly credit any of this. Though as a degree of reasoning started to enter her brain she realised that he must be referring to the fact that Khalil Rashwan would have gone home to his father nursing a swollen jaw. In a flash she was on her feet and holding her robe close to her, grabbing at what pride she could find to say hotly, 'It wasn't me who hit Khalil Rashw...'

'No—you were satisfied to lead him on—right up to your bedroom door!' Thane scorched her ears. And while she was swallowing that, 'Well, I've news for you, Miss Harding,' he told her acidly. 'Beacon Oil doesn't do business that way.' Shaken rigid by what he had just said, Joss momentarily lost her grip on her housecoat. She saw a pulse beat in his temple as her robe parted at her breast, but she was totally unprepared for the fresh shock of his curt, 'Consider yourself no longer in the company's employ!'

She was staring after him open-mouthed when, with that, he went towards the door. Before he could open it, though, she was rocketing outraged from her shock. Perhaps it had taken the shock of what he had just said to negate the other helping of shock he had dealt her. But whatever the cause, she was instantly furious, and not likely to keep quiet about it.

'You can't dismiss me!' she shrieked, more enraged than ever that he was daring to serve *her* with the same dismissal treatment he had served Paula Ingram. 'I resign,' she spat. 'You can take your job and...' Her voice faded as she realised she was talking to the air. Thane had gone and had slammed her door shut behind him.

How could he? The swine, the diabolical swine! Who did he think he was, to tell her that she was dismissed? How could a man hold her in his arms one minute, the way he had done, and then tell her in the next that she was no longer in the company's employ?

For all of five shattered minutes, Joss could think of nothing else. Then suddenly, as pride arrived in great all-consuming measure, she was galvanised into action. In no time at all, spurred on by fury and outraged pride, she, who had never in her life been dismissed from a job, was furiously throwing things into her case and getting out of there.

'Taxi?' asked a taxi-driver the moment she put her nose outside the hotel.

'The airport,' she told him and, handing him her case, she did not first agree the fare as some weeks ago Baz Barton had advised. To her way of thinking any price would be agreeable so long as it took her far enough away from that monstrous swine Thane Addison.

She was still in high fury when the taxi-driver handed her back her case at Luxor airport. Who the *hell* did Thane Addison think he was? she railed as she went to find out the chance of a flight to Alexandria.

A flight to Alexandria was out, she discovered, though the next plane out was a delayed flight to Cairo. She supposed the sandstorm must have something to do with the delay, but somehow she suddenly felt it more imperative that she get out of Luxor with all speed than to worry where her plane landed. She booked a flight to Cairo.

The plane had taken off, with her on board, before it occurred to her that perhaps she wasn't thinking very rationally. Because as her thoughts turned to the next step, that of taking a flight from Cairo home to England, she remembered that quite a few of her belongings were back at the apartment in Alexandria.

A few seconds later, however, she experienced a moment's rebellion, and suddenly she was of the opinion that any clothes and belongings she had in Alexandria could jolly well stay there. She was going home—to England.

Although Joss remained of the view that she would not return to Alexandria to pick up the remainder of her things, the rest of her rebellion was short-lived. She tried hard to stay angry by telling herself that Thane Addison really was a swine—where had his famous diplomacy been when he'd taken a swing at Khalil Rashwan? That was what she'd like to know.

It was the simple fact of a stewardess coming and bringing round cheese sandwiches that triggered a weakening in Joss's harsh thoughts. Only then did she remember that she hadn't had any dinner. Which memory brought on another memory, the memory of how she had been going to dine with Thane that evening, of her excitement, and of looking forward to him calling for her.

A dry sob rose up in her throat, she choked it back, and blinked several times. She wouldn't cry, she would not. Oh, how could he have acted towards her the way that he had? How could the fates have been so unfair as to allow her to spend such a sublime day, when they had waiting in store for her such utter misery?

The flight to Cairo took fifty minutes, and, having landed and collected her case from the carousel, Joss decided to go and see about a flight to England. Her thoughts were still on Thane as she went—this time, on how he had threatened her with dismissal at the very outset.

He hadn't dismissed her for falling in love with him— that he had no idea of how she felt about him was the only bright spot in any of this. No, what he'd dismissed her for was because she'd ruined his weeks of solid work, which had culminated in him and Khalil's father initialling that contract. Thane had...

Abruptly, her thoughts shut off. Suddenly as the words 'that contract' played back in her mind she stood stock still and let her case fall to the ground. Yazid Rashwan might in his anger tear up his copy of that initialled contract, but there was another copy of that document—and she had it—in her suitcase!

Feeling totally stunned, Joss picked up her case and reeled to a chair to try and get her head together. Several thoughts began to crowd her mind at once then, one of them being that while Yazid Rashwan might well be furious with Thane for hitting his beloved son on the jaw, Yazid was still the same man of honour, wasn't he?

Even so, even if after due consideration he did not tear up his copy of the contract, she just couldn't pretend that she did not have Beacon's copy of that highly confidential document in her possession. Dismissed she might be, though she preferred to believe she had resigned, but no efficient secretary worth the name would just dump a document like that, no matter how they had been treated. Well, maybe they would, she thought a moment later, but not if they were in love with the swine who had dismissed them.

Joss faced the fact that she was feeling very confused. What she was not confused about, however, was that she did not want to see Thane again. Never would she forget his 'You've been giving me the green light all day'—nor the way she'd shown him just how much she hadn't been giving him the green light, by putting up no more than minimal resistance when he had taken her in his arms.

She turned her thoughts away from such a painful memory, but, much as she shied away from having to see Thane again, she realised that she could not return to England without handing that document over to someone.

Once she had reached that conclusion, the decision seemed made for her. She left the airport building in search of a taxi, and planned it out as she went. She would deliver that contract to Malcolm Cooper at the Cairo office tomorrow. She would ask Malcolm to let Thane know that he had it, and also ask Malcolm to keep it in his safe until Thane either called for it, or sent someone for it.

'Taxi?' a fatherly-looking Egyptian man enquired.

Joss, with her thoughts on making for some hotel, since she couldn't stay at the airport overnight, nor could she camp out on the office doorstep until someone arrived to let her in, gave the driver her case and unthinkingly said the first thing to come into her head.

'Giza,' she told him for her destination, and realised that her head wasn't so clear as she had thought. Though when the driver, without turning a hair, closed the door on her and started up his taxi, she shrugged and thought that a hotel in Giza was as good a place as any.

He seemed a talkative driver, and spoke English to some degree. But when at any other time Joss might have been ready to pass a few pleasantries with him, she was starting to feel used up. Talk between them therefore consisted only of her telling him that she wanted to go to a good standard of hotel, and of him replying that he thought he knew one which would suit.

'You are on holiday?' he did try, but lapsed into silence after her monosyllabic reply.

'No,' she told him affably.

It was just over half an hour later, when he pulled up outside a hotel in Giza, when Joss started to realise just how confused she must be. Because, when she had had the ideal opportunity back at the airport to book her flight to England, she only then realised that she had not done so.

'Thank you very much,' she told the driver as he carried her luggage inside the hotel, and, just in case she had hurt his feelings by being such a silent passenger, she gave him a generous tip.

'Enjoy your stay here!' he beamed, and left her to it, and Joss approached the reception desk with her fingers crossed that she would be *able* to stay here. With her mind so elsewhere occupied, she just hadn't given thought to the fact that they might not have a room to spare.

Her worry proved groundless, however, for regardless of the hour—for it was by then two in the morning—the very pleasant man on duty seemed not to be able to do enough for her. 'Of course, madam,' he replied, with his dark-eyed glance on her creamy complexion and ash-blonde hair. 'How long will you be staying?'

'For one night only,' she told him, and, since he seemed to want to be helpful, 'Is it possible for me to book a flight to England from here?'

'For you—I am sure,' he smiled.

Half an hour later, given a hiccup or two in the booking of her flight, Joss was shown up to a room on the third floor, her flight booked for that afternoon.

A glance at her watch showed it was half-past two, and although she felt weary but not sleepy, she supposed she had better get into bed. Unstrapping her case, she took out her toilet articles and nightclothes and then, what was now becoming 'that wretched contract' in her mind, she extracted her leather document case from the folds of her cream silk dress, and checked the contents. Everything was there, she noted, and she put the document wallet back in her case and closed the lid. Then she washed, changed and got into bed.

She put the light out—nightmare thoughts crept in. She put the light on again, and lay there wide awake, her head abuzz with all that had so catastrophically happened. She hadn't led Khalil on to that extent, despite what Thane said. It was Thane himself who had more or less told her not to offend Khalil. Oh, it just wasn't fair, it just wasn't!

She fell into a light doze, wishing she could hate Thane for longer than short bursts. But she loved him, that love seeming to be without pride. For even after the way he had spoken to her, she still loved him.

Joss drifted to full wakefulness twenty minutes later, and twenty minutes after that she made more determined efforts to get some sleep by turning out her bedside lamp.

Her sleep was a little deeper that time, and a little longer. Though it was still dark outside when at just after quarter to five she was wakened from her slumbers by the town's faithful being called to prayer by a disembodied voice echoing from a loudspeaker over the rooftops.

Joss sat up, glad of the company. Somewhere a dog barked and a camel made its presence known, and, by then so wide awake that she knew there was no chance of getting back to sleep again, she consigned herself to sit and listen.

All the while the prayers and chanting went on she was making gallant efforts to push Thane from her mind. When shortly after five the chanting stopped, she had no chance to concentrate on anything else, and Thane, Thane, Thane whirled round in her brain.

Which was why, when at fifteen minutes past five the telephone on her bedside rang, she was glad of the distraction—any distraction would have been welcomed. She picked it up, knowing in advance that someone must have booked an alarm call for five-fifteen and that the night porter, or whoever attended to such matters, must have got the room number wrong.

She had meant, when she spoke, to quote her room number, but what she actually said, her wide-awake tone belying that she needed any alarm call, was 'Hello?'

Then she almost collapsed with shock and thought that, with having Thane so much on her mind, she must have gone over the edge. Because the voice that answered was the voice of the man she loved! Incredibly, it was—Thane!

'Joss,' he stated evenly, 'I'd like to see you.'

Thane! He...! What...? She took a deep breath, and suddenly her heart leapt—Thane wanted to see her. 'I'm...' she began, then, like lead, her soaring spirits plummeted. Oh, what an idiot she was! Of course Thane wanted to see her—though not her at all really. More precisely, he'd remembered that she had that contract, and he'd have made contact with the devil himself in order to have that contract he'd worked so hard on restored to him. Pride, which she had thought had deserted her, then charged to the rescue, and somehow she had made her voice as cool as his had been as she told him airily, 'That might prove a little difficult.'

He didn't like her tone, she knew he didn't, it was all there in the one sharp word he rapped back at her. 'Why?' he asked tersely.

'With you in Luxor and me in Cairo...' She broke off as only then did the magnitude of what was happening strike her. Heavens above—how on earth had Thane known she had left Luxor—that she had flown to Cairo? Or even, more astonishingly, which hotel she had booked into?

'In point of fact, I'm not in Luxor,' his voice came again when it appeared he thought he'd waited long enough for her to finish what she had started to say.

'Y-you're—not?'

'No,' he replied shortly.

'You're in Cairo?' she guessed, hoping with all she had that she was wrong, because it would really be much better if she did not see him again. Her way of getting that contract to him was much the better idea.

'No,' he replied again, and for all of a second Joss breathed a sigh of relief. But that was before he added coolly, 'I'm in Giza.'

Suddenly her hand was gripping tightly on to the phone. Thane was here—in Giza! All at once her hands went moist, then in contrast her throat went dry. And as she went to speak her voice came out sounding husky when she put the question which she was beginning to think she knew the answer to before she asked it. That question, 'Which—h-hotel?'

'The same one you're in,' he replied.

'The same...' she echoed, her voice fading—she was shaken, even if he had confirmed what she had started to suspect.

'I'm along the corridor from you,' Thane told her, his tone taking on a crisp note, when, businesslike and a man with never a minute to spare, he went on abruptly, 'I've a meeting at eight—is it convenient if I come and see you now?'

Now! His forthright question sent Joss, who had never before knowing him dithered in her life, into something of a dither. No, no, no, said her head. Oh, yes, said her heart. She remembered how he had been the last time she had seen him, his accusation that she had given him the green light, and never, said her pride. Against that, though, was the fact that he had laboured hard and long in pulling off that contract. What more natural than that he should chase after her to get it? It would only take a moment to hand it over to him; she didn't even have to say one single word to him.

'Well?' he barked shortly, clearly not liking to be kept holding on while she made up her mind.

'Quite convenient!' she snapped, and slammed the phone down.

She was glad to feel angry with him, although unfortunately she could not sustain that anger. In seconds after slamming down the phone she went absolutely haywire. There was no sign of the unflappable Miss Josslyn Harding then as, leaping out of bed, she didn't know what to do first—run a comb through her hair, get into her housecoat or get the contract Thane was coming for out of her case.

Before she had done more than button up her housecoat and extract the wallet from her suitcase, though, and all before she was ready, she heard Thane's light tap on her door. She supposed she should be grateful that he was considerate of the other residents. Thane being Thane, it wouldn't have surprised her if he hadn't taken out his frustration that she'd waltzed off with the contract by thumping on the wood panelling. Hastily, taking up the leather wallet as she went, she sped to the door before he should get fed up with waiting and start to do just that.

At the door, however, her nerve momentarily disappeared, and she had to take a very deep breath before she reached down to the door-handle.

Her deep breath was meant to be a steadying one, but it was a waste of time. For as soon as the door was open, and she stood faced with Thane, her colour flared and her legs went like jelly. Oh, how dear to her he was, she fretted, as she looked at the tallness of him, and observed that he was dressed in shirt and slacks. He seemed newly shaven, she thought, but there was a look of strain about his eyes that worried her. Those eyes, though, seemed to be dissecting every aspect of her face, but although she knew he had come for the contents of the leather wallet, he was making no move to take it from her.

As yet, neither of them had spoken a word, but suddenly, as her high colour faded, Joss saw unhappily that there was no need for words. Everything that had needed saying between them had been said.

Wordlessly she lifted the document case and pushed it at him. Wordlessly his eyes left hers and he glanced down at the wallet she was offering. Though when she thought it must be some relief to him that the company's confidence had not been broken and that he could rest easy now that he had retrieved the contract, he suddenly absolutely astounded her. For instead of taking the document case from her—which surely he must have recognised from having seen it before—he did no such thing. But, raising a hand, instead he pushed it back at her.

Even more astounding, though alarming was more appropriate, Joss felt, was the way he then unceremoniously pushed his way into her room, and as she stepped back he deliberately closed the door.

Then, with his eyes going over her from the tip of her tousled blonde head to the toes of her mule-attired feet, he took the wallet from her and tossed it on to the bed. 'I didn't come for *that*!' he clipped, and suddenly, as all at once she noted the dangerous glint in his eyes, her insides started to tremble. She did not know why then he had come, but she had never known him sound so tough—or so determined!

CHAPTER NINE

NEVER more did Joss desperately need some composure, but as she stared at Thane all she felt was one agitated mass of inner turmoil. Eventually, however, she managed to find her voice, but it was only a trifle as cool as she had wanted to sound. 'You—might have said. You could have saved yourself a visit.'

'I—wanted to—see you,' Thane replied, and although he could not be meaning anything personal, what he answered nevertheless caused her heart to beat faster.

'It—er—must have been important—for you to follow me from Luxor,' she retorted, still trying to sound cool but, with Thane now holding her stare and refusing to let her look away, having the hardest work in the world just to think clearly. 'Oh . . .!' she exclaimed as one clear thought did occur to her. 'You must have been coming to Cairo anyway, so . . .'

She broke off when he made an impatient movement, though he did not contradict that he had been planning to come to Cairo anyway, but agreed, 'It was important, and still is.'

Which, as far as she could see, just had to mean that he was there, despite what he'd said, in connection with that contract which now reposed on her bed. Managing at last to tear her eyes away from his, she glanced to the leather wallet, 'You're sure you didn't come for that contract?' she queried, never having known him tell a lie, but feeling too confused suddenly to find any other answers.

Having looked away from Thane, though, her glance went shooting back at him when, after a second or two of silence, he told her quietly, 'I came—among other reasons—to apologise.'

The 'other reasons' passed her by. '*You*—apologise?' she queried in amazement, and then found the stiffening she needed, as sarcastically she requested, 'Pardon me while I faint!'

'Am I so bad?' he enquired.

'How long have you got?' she answered spiritedly, and was weakened again when, most surprisingly, she saw the corners of his mouth twitch. Swiftly she went in search of more stiffening. 'So what, *in particular*,' she found more acid, 'are you apologising for?'

His amused look had not stayed around very long, she noticed, for his expression was tough again as though her continued acid tone was starting to needle him. And, as she supposed she might have expected, it didn't take him a second to vanquish her tart tongue. 'Not for damn near seducing you!' he bit sharply, and as pink flared in her cheeks as she was reminded of how small her show of resistance had been once he'd taken her in his arms, he startled her by groaning, 'Oh, confound it, Joss, have you no...?' Abruptly, he broke off, and, even more startling as far as she was concerned, she could have sworn that Thane, who she knew put his signature to deals worth millions without turning a hair, seemed strangely—nervous. 'Look,' he said after a moment, 'can we sit down?'

'It won't take that long, surely?' she replied, loving him, hating him, but above all afraid of giving away the fact that her love for him made her hatred puny by comparison.

'You're not going anywhere for some hours yet,' he retorted, and somehow she had a feeling that he not only knew—when she had told no one—of her plan to be at Beacon House, Cairo, at nine, but also the time of her flight to England that day. Which, all in all, made her realise that if he could know what thoughts went on in her head, she would be wise to be doubly wary of him.

Somehow she managed to shrug as though it was neither here nor there to her. But, needing to hide her expression from him for a moment, she turned and made for a pair of small easy chairs in the corner of the room, which were separated by a low table placed between them.

'You were apologising, I believe,' she murmured when they were both seated, hoping with all she had as his eyes rested on her that she looked more relaxed than she felt. How she wished there had been time to fling some clothes on—not that to merely hand over that wallet, as she had thought, had in her opinion necessitated getting her best outfit out of the wardrobe. She saw his eyes move to her tousled hair, and wished too that she'd found time to pull a comb through it.

'I *was* apologising,' Thane took up after several moments of not saying anything, but just looking at her. 'I was way out of line in accusing you of leading Khalil Rashwan on when—short of telling him to go and take a running jump, and given that dealing with his crush on you called for some tactful handling—you acted in the only way your loyalty to the company would have you act.'

Crazily her heart gave an upward leap that Thane should now speak to her in full understanding of the difficulties she had faced. Against that, though, was her hurt at the way he had laid into her. Was she such a pathetic creature that, having now received his approbation for her actions, she should smile sweetly and tell him to think nothing more of it? She had to live with herself, didn't she?

'In point of fact, I quite liked Khalil.' Joss at last found the cool note she had wanted earlier. She saw Thane frown, though whether from her tone or what she had said, she didn't know. But he wasn't backward when it came to cutting her off, for as she took a breath to go on he was rapidly there to have his say.

'It didn't look to me as though you were liking him too well when he made a grab for you!' he told her curtly.

'That was different,' she snapped, not too thrilled to have that thrown up at her. 'Well, thank you for your apology,' she went on swiftly, and, taking it that this interview was over, made to get to her feet.

She hurriedly sat down, however, when Thane rose too and stayed her by stretching out his hands to her hands. 'I haven't finished yet,' he told her. 'In fact, I've barely begun.'

'In that case——' She sank into her chair once more, nerves again starting to bite as she snatched her hands away from his tingling touch. She felt a mass of agitation again, and longed for calm as he retook his seat and eyed her levelly. 'Am I to assume,' she said swiftly, 's-since you haven't finished yet, that you regret dismissing me for leading Khalil Rashwan on—right up to my bedroom door, I think you said?' she reminded him, and felt heartily glad to find the tart edge she wanted was there. 'Beacon Oil don't do business that way, I think you also said,' she added for full sarcastic and non-doormat measure.

To her surprise, though, when she fully expected that Thane might have something much more wounding to throw at her in reply, there was not a trace of sarcasm in his answer. Indeed, he seemed to agree that she was right to say what she had. 'I deserve to have that slammed back at me,' he said quietly. Then, after a moment's pause, 'Though there were—extenuating circumstances,' he went on slowly. Then, without pausing to tell her what these extenuating circumstances were, 'Of course you're not dismissed,' he stated. 'You're far too valuable to the company.'

Conversely, Joss did not want to be valuable to the *company*—she wanted to be valuable to *him*. 'I'm still valuable to the company, even though I've lost you that contract?' she queried, trying hard to adopt an uncaring note.

'Lost it?' he questioned.

'I know we've still got our copy,' she replied snappily, throwing him an exasperated look, 'and I know that because of its content it's still a highly confidential document. But if Yazid Rashwan has torn up his copy...'

'What makes you think he'd do anything of that sort?' Thane cut in coolly, and at that, Joss lost control of her temper.

'You're impossible!' she exploded, and raced on hotly, 'And I quote "Thanks to you and your wanton behaviour you've ruined what has taken months to achieve"!'

'Oh, hell!' Thane swore softly, just as though it did not please him to have his remarks quoted back at him. Then, giving her a level look, 'I can explain all that,' he said, but did not do so, but went on, 'It might relieve your mind to know that before I left Luxor I took a phone call from a very concerned Yazid Rashwan.'

'Concerned?' she queried, and, her interest taken, she forgot that Thane had not explained the reason for his offensive remarks.

Thane nodded, then continued, 'Apparently Khalil went home and told him how with a few—sharp words— I'd turfed him out of your room.'

Joss recalled how Thane had let fly with something in Arabic at Khalil, but that wasn't all she recalled. 'From what I remember,' she told him coolly, 'you hurled, rather than merely "turfed", Khalil out.'

'He deserved it!' he clipped.

'I hope his father appreciated that fact!' she retorted tartly, and was a little open-mouthed at his reply.

'He did,' he told her solemnly. 'His reason for ringing was to tell me how Khalil, while not realising how things were—with you and me—was trying to get——'

'Things between you and me!' she exclaimed, and wished she hadn't. She knew as well as Thane that there was nothing between them—not on his side, anyway—so all she'd done was to bring attention to something she was very much nervous of discussing lest she slipped up in some small way.

'You'll forgive me, I hope, Joss,' he said, his eyes steady on hers as she tried to cover the fact that just his using her first name had made her feel soft about him inside again, 'but, while helping Khalil on his way, I told him that—you were my woman.'

Blankly she stared at him. Even as her heart went wild inside her, she made gigantic efforts to keep her composure as she tried to reason why Thane, given the fury he had been in, should tell Khalil that she was his woman.

Her heart was still on a dizzy merry-go-round—until suddenly she lighted upon the answer. Immediately, her racing heartbeats slowed. Thane would do anything to save that contract. Even while he was furious, his clear-thinking mind would lose none of its sharpness where that contract was concerned.

'Naturally, you'd have to tell him something to excuse hitting him,' she said aloofly. 'Naturally, too...' His dark look made her break off.

'I didn't *have* to tell him...' Suddenly *he* broke off, and most peculiarly Joss thought he looked strangely nervous again. She dismissed the notion as idiotic, but observed that he took a long breath before going on. Then, as though all at once wanting it quickly out of the way, he told her swiftly. 'When Khalil Rashwan got his head back together he, according to Yazid, while trying to get over his disappointment that you were "spoken for", became fearful that he'd offended against some British custom, and might have ruined the hours of work his father had put in on the contract.'

Joss's mouth was definitely open as Thane came to an end. 'So Yazid Rashwan rang you, to check that *you* hadn't changed *your* mind about the contract!' she exclaimed when what he had just said had fully sunk in.

'That's about it,' he confirmed, and Joss gave him a disgruntled look of disgust.

'Huh!' she scorned. 'If you fell in a dung heap you'd come up smelling of roses!' She saw his lips twitch again, but she wasn't feeling very friendly to him just then— he'd no right to have so much going for him. 'You'll tell me next, of course, that, with the certainty that you hadn't after all lost the contract, you felt, since you'd planned to be in Cairo today for your eight o'clock meeting, that you'd be magnanimous and let me know, in person, that I wasn't dismissed after all!' Suddenly she discovered that this man was just *too* much, and that she had worked herself up into quite a temper. 'Well, I've news for you, Mr No-please-and-very-little-thank-you Addison, I wouldn't work for you or Beacon Oil now if...'

'For lord's sake! What did I say?' he chopped in, but Joss had spent hours and hours in mental torment over him, and she wasn't ready to cool down—not now that she had let go.

'You've said more than enough!' she erupted, and, not deigning to go again over the insults he had served her, 'Had Yazid Rashwan not telephoned you tonight—last night,' she hastily amended, 'to let you know that that contract was safe, you'd not have given me a second's thought. You certainly wouldn't have tried to contact me. You'd have left Luxor without giving me another thought. You'd have...'

'Hell's bells, will you shut up?' Thane roared, about the only way he could get in.

Joss blinked, but having been so rudely interrupted caused her to break her tirade, and then start to panic that she might, in all she had said, have somehow revealed the fact that, desperate for any crumb, she had wanted him to give her another thought.

'So?' she challenged belligerently.

'So,' he said harshly, 'if you'll let me get a word in edgeways, I'll tell you that of course I thought of you. Ye gods, woman, I'd been searching Luxor for you *before* Yazid's call came through!'

Astounded by what he had just said, Joss just sat and gaped at him. Then, 'You'd been—searching... *Before* Yazid rang, you...' Her voice tailed off.

But if her tone was much more subdued than it had been, then Thane's tone too was very much quieter as he told her, 'You gave me one hell of a fright lighting out like that.'

'I—d-did?' she questioned, and then, desperately trying to get herself of one piece, 'You surely didn't think I'd so taken your remarks to heart that I'd thrown myself in the Nile?' She saw his glance on her become a trace speculative, and again started to panic that she might have revealed that anything offensive he might have to say did have the power to wound her deeply.

To her relief, though, he made no comment on that score, but replied after a moment or two of just looking at her, 'No, I didn't think that,' and then opened up, 'After I—left you—your room, I took myself off for a walk. Many thoughts went through my head during that walk,' he told her, 'but suffice it to say that my first action on my return was to go to your room.'

'I—see,' Joss said slowly, and realised then that Thane must have cooled down on his walk and, having done so, must have then have been plagued by his innate sense of fairness—that sense of fairness making him decide to come to her room to apologise. 'But I wasn't there,' she went on, 'so you . . .' She broke off and looked solemnly into his steady grey eyes. Somehow she just couldn't credit that he had, as he'd said, been searching Luxor for her.

'So I began looking for you,' he took up. 'We'd been going to dine, I recalled belatedly, then I realised that, you being you, you'd probably rather starve than break bread with me again after the way I'd behaved. Which, to my logical mind, meant that since you had to eat that you would, in all likelihood, take a taxi to some other hotel rather than risk having to share the same air if I was eating in the hotel we were staying in.'

As she looked at him, her resistance to him began to crumble. By the sound of it, he had given her more than a moment's thought. 'I forgot that I hadn't eaten,' she confessed quietly.

'Oh, my dear,' Thane said softly, and straight away her heart was on a merry-go-round again. 'Were you so upset by me that . . . ?'

'Grief!' she scoffed swiftly, and was unsure whether or not her bluff of being entirely unaffected by him had come off.

But Thane was going on, and that small moment of danger was past, as he continued, 'I took a taxi to check the most likely hotels, then returned to try your room again.' Joss's eyes were widening in her face as she heard the trouble he had gone to in looking for her. But it did not end there. 'Then, when you didn't answer your door, I went down to reception to enquire if anyone had seen you. It was then I was told that your room key had been handed in, and that one of them could clearly remember seeing you with your suitcase.'

'Good heavens!' Joss exclaimed in surprise. The hotel they had stayed in had been a busy one. 'With everyone coming and going all the time, you wouldn't think anyone would remember...'

'It was a male of the species,' Thane broke in, making her heart flutter. 'You're not so easily overlooked, Joss.'

'Oh,' she murmured, and knew her feelings for him were getting the better of her. 'So what did you do?' she made herself ask a little stiffly. 'After one of the hotel staff had said...'

'What would I do?' he questioned. 'I took the key and checked your room for myself.'

Her eyes went even wider at that. 'You—er—found me gone, my clothes gone?'

He nodded. 'But not a clue anywhere to where you *had* gone. I was in my room throwing my things into my case when Yazid Rashwan rang.'

'Ah,' said Joss, and thought then that she had the whole picture. 'You realised that you'd spent enough time searching for me and that if you wasted any more you'd miss your flight to Cairo?'

'At that stage,' he replied, his eyes nowhere but on her, 'I didn't know if I'd be flying to Cairo, Alexandria or where the hell I'd be flying.'

'But your meeting!' she reminded him. 'The meeting you said you have in Cairo at eight o'clock this morning.'

'I lied about that,' Thane owned, and as far as she could tell he didn't appear to look in the least bit sorry.

'You—lied?'

'What else should I do?' he enquired. 'I'd been lucky so far in finding you. When you answered your phone sounding wide awake, I decided that I hadn't been through what I'd been through just so that you should tell me you'd see me at a more civilised hour.'

All that he'd been through? Joss could only think he must mean the trouble he'd been to to track her down. Though, since it seemed that he had no appointment in Cairo that morning, surely it had to mean that he—had *purposely*—followed her to Cairo! Suddenly her heart was beating rapidly again, and she knew then that she wanted, most urgently, to hear everything he had to tell her. Because—and she owned that she was feeling more than a degree confused—surely, when Thane could have easily telexed her pretty well anywhere in the world to tell her that he considered her still in the company's employ, he had come after her personally, meant that there was more to it than that. Didn't it? She remembered the marvellous day she had shared with him—until Khalil had come on the scene—and she swallowed hard on a dry throat. Good or bad, she wanted Thane to tell her the other reasons why he had come after her.

'You—er—said you'd been lucky?' she questioned, her voice sounding suddenly husky despite all her efforts to the contrary.

'Thank God for that sandstorm!' Thane said on a heartfelt note, and when she just sat and stared uncomprehendingly he explained, 'But for the luck of that sandstorm affecting flying schedules, I wouldn't have a clue where you'd flown to. When I started asking questions at the airport it soon became evident that because of the readjusted time-tables, the only flight you could have taken in the time scale of your leaving the hotel had to be the one to Cairo.'

'Good heavens!' Joss exclaimed again, though her tone was fainter this time. It seemed incredible that Thane had done such detective work about her. 'So you really did fly to Cairo after me?'

'And spent most of the flight wondering if you'd cooled down sufficiently to remember that you still had the contract, or if you were too mad, still hating my guts.'

'I—er——' she murmured, and realised that to tell him she'd been more hurt than mad would not do at all. 'I didn't remember the contract until my plane had landed,' she told him, then all at once, as her logical thinking started to stir, her spirits hit rock bottom again. 'That's why you followed me!' she declared suddenly. 'You knew I'd still got the contract and . . .' She broke off, shaken, as she saw from the furious expression that crossed his face and knew she had just made him exceedingly angry.

'Have you not been listening to a word I've said?' he roared on an explosion of anger. 'To hell with that contract—it's got nothing to do with why I'm here, nor did I give it a thought when I was searching Luxor for you! In fact, had Yazid Rashwan not telephoned about it, I doubt if I should have remembered it at all,' he blazed on. 'The only reason it stayed in my head during my journey here,' he informed her furiously, 'was that, to my mind, so much hinged on your remembering that you still had it.'

'I don't see how,' Joss told him stiffly, not caring to be roared at by him or anyone else.

'Then try this!' he rapped toughly. 'I'd checked your room pretty thoroughly when I was looking for you, but

it wasn't until after Yazid's phone call that I realised
that had you left that contract for me I'd have seen it—
likewise, had you torn it to shreds and dumped it in your
paper-bin, I'd have spotted it there too.'

'You thought I might have torn it up!' Joss exclaimed
in astonishment, a little shaken to see that her surprised
exclamation appeared to have neutralised Thane's anger
with her. For suddenly he smiled.

'I wouldn't have blamed you,' he replied gently, and
while her heart flipped and she did what she could in
the way of getting herself under control from the havoc
just his smile and his gentleness had created in her, he
went on, 'To my way of thinking, it seemed a pretty safe
bet that you'd flown to Cairo, but it was also a pretty
safe bet that, since you hadn't hung about Luxor airport
waiting for the Alexandria flight, you'd no intention of
returning there. Which in turn had to mean that what
you did intend to do was to take the first flight out of
Cairo to England, when for all I knew you might
disappear to stay with people I'd never heard of, when
it could be an age before I could find you.' Joss stared
at him incredulously—was he saying that he would have
followed her to England? 'That was,' he went on,
'unless...'

'Un-l-less?' she prompted, in love with him, fasci-
nated by the way his mind worked, but above all feeling
so strung up that she wanted him to go on, and quickly.

For a moment or two Thane said nothing, but just
rested his eyes on her as if just the sight of her made
him feel good to be alive. Her heart was thundering
against her ribs when he suddenly seemed to collect
himself, then replied, 'Unless you'd remembered that
most confidential of documents. I haven't worked with
you these past weeks, Joss, without learning that as well
as having a shocking temper...' he broke off briefly when

she looked as though she was going to argue the point, but when her lips stayed firmly closed, however, he resumed, 'you also happen to be one of the most loyal and efficient working partners a man could wish for.'

'Now he tells me!' Joss, while thrilled at his 'working partners' terminology, found that this time she could not take what he said without comment.

'You shouldn't need telling,' he rebuked her, a trace of good humour lurking at the corners of his mouth. 'I scoured Cairo airport for you, Josslyn Harding,' he enlightened her severely. 'When I couldn't find you, I had to pin all my hopes on your sense of duty, to the company, if not to me, winning through.'

'You—er—calculated that if I remembered in time that I hadn't yet given that document back to you, I wouldn't leave Cairo until I'd made sure it was in safe hands?'

'I wanted to see you, dear Joss,' he told her quietly, and while her eyes went saucer-wide and her mouth went dry and she started to tremble, he added, 'Which is why I had to hope with all my heart that, having remembered the contract, you would feel you couldn't trust it to the post, but would take it personally to the Cairo office as soon as it opened.'

'You . . .' she swallowed hard when her voice came out sounding more of a whisper than anything else. 'You—um—thought that you'd—er—meet me at Beacon House when . . .' Her voice faded.

'It was my intention to be there before you,' Thane took up, his eyes never leaving her face. 'But that was before I realised that I was so impatient to see you that I couldn't wait that long.'

'You couldn't?' she choked, and just sat staring at him as he shook his head and then confided,

'I raced round several hotels in Cairo checking to see if you were booked in. Then I suddenly remembered how you'd had a yearning to see the Pyramids. It was a long shot, but I abandoned my attempts to find you in Cairo and tried Giza instead.'

'Well...!' escaped Joss on a stunned breath of sound. Then, her voice strengthening, she felt she just had to tell him, 'To be honest, I was a bit all over the place—and wasn't thinking about the Pyramids when I told the taxi-driver that I wanted to go to Giza.'

For some seconds Thane stared at her as if he had taken quite some heart from the fact that, for a good long while after their row, she had still been all over the place. But, instead of putting the onus on her to tell him why that should be, he smiled, that gentle smile she was beginning to love, and told her, 'It doesn't matter, I found you.' His smile faded as he continued, 'But having found you, having booked myself in—a few doors up from you—I discovered that I couldn't settle to wait until daylight to see you.'

'You w-were awake when the call to prayer started?'

'My dear, I hadn't been to sleep,' he told her. 'Nor, when I began to wonder if the noise had awakened you, could I find it possible to wait any longer. When I rang your room and heard you sounding fully awake, I was at one and the same time encouraged that—by the sound of it—you couldn't sleep either; only to know myself for a fool to think that anyone could sleep with all that chanting going on.'

Looking at him, Joss thought she would soon collapse under the strain of the tension she was suddenly under. Nervously she licked her bottom lip, and then she just had to ask, 'Encouraged—why, Thane?'

'Don't you know yet?' he asked quietly, and Joss grew very afraid that she had got it wrong and that her normal intelligence might have led her into an entirely false avenue.

However, she did find enough courage to begin, 'If it's not the contract that's important to y-you...' when suddenly her voice failed her, and she could go no further.

Which was when Thane, that look of strain evident in his eyes again, manfully took over. 'If it's not the contract which is so important to me,' he said, his grey eyes holding hers and reading what they could from her tense expression, 'then what is so very, very important to me that I've hared from Luxor to find you must, my very dear Joss, be you.'

'Oh!' she exclaimed softly, wanting to cry, wanting to launch herself at him, wanting above all to be held safe in his arms and for him to tell her that she really could believe what he was telling her.

'What does that "Oh!" signify?' he asked, his tone suddenly gritty, and sounding very much as though he was bracing himself to hear the worst.

Joss swallowed on her dry throat. 'It means,' she told him nervously, 'that—I'm—scared.'

'Of me?' he exclaimed abruptly, clearly appalled that she should be afraid of him.

'Of what you're *not* saying,' she replied swiftly.

'Of what I'm not...' he began to repeat, then suddenly stopped, and then, letting go what seemed to her to be a long-pent-up breath, 'I've just been telling you—for the lord knows how long—that I love you very much, Josslyn Harding. Are you now going to tell me that you, whom I've seen fully and quickly grasp the most complicated of issues, haven't worked that out yet?'

'A woman—likes to have these things spelled out,' she told him modestly, if shakily, as her heart pounded away so loudly that she was sure he must hear it.

'Likes?' he took up the one word. 'You wouldn't give a man such encouragement without meaning it, would you?'

Joss almost asked him what sort of a woman he thought she was, but a glance at his stressed expression told her that he was never more earnest. 'No,' she said simply, 'I wouldn't.'

His answer was to stand up. Then he held out his arms to her. 'Come over here and say that,' he commanded her softly.

Quietly she left her chair. 'Thane!' she breathed his name, and as he reached out for her and gently pulled her into his arms, it was all she said for quite some minutes.

Then, after long moments of holding her close up against his heart, of leaning back so that he could look into her face, and of then gently, and oh, so tenderly, kissing her, Thane put her a little way away from him, and while still keeping his hands on her shoulders, 'Oh, my darling!' he murmured, and for the first time since she had known him, he seemed choked, and lost for words. Then, 'I won't ask you how in the name of good fortune you've come to care for me, but since I shouldn't mind having it spelled out either—is there anything you want to tell *me*?'

It seemed totally unbelievable to Joss that he should need to hear her say that she loved him, but, remembering how not all that long ago she had been nervous to believe he was saying that he loved her, she breathed shakily, 'Oh, Thane, I do so love you!'

He gave an exultant cry of triumph, and suddenly she was back in his arms again and he was raining tender loving kisses all over her face. Many more long minutes ticked by as he held her close against his heart. Then gradually he pulled back from her again.

His eyes were devouring her loving face. 'The torment you've caused me, dear love!' he whispered. 'The jealousy I've known since you, ash-blonde and female, and not at all what I wanted, arrived in Cairo, and coolly told me you were the replacement secretary.'

'Jealousy?' she questioned, positively adoring him.

'We have so much to talk about,' he smiled, and, quite clearly wanting her as close to him as possible, he moved her with him and took her to sit with him in one of the small easy chairs—the only room available for her being—on his lap. Then, securing her in his arms, 'You can have no idea of how all at sea I've been about you, young woman,' he informed her mock-seriously.

'I haven't,' she admitted, then, sending him a smile which he seemed to relish, 'but I should like to,' she told him.

'Minx!' he accused. 'Adorable minx,' and to please her he related, 'We started off by rowing the day we met. I, with the recent example of Paula Ingram, and how a friendly look can be misread, before me, dared to warn you against taking a fancy to me. What, in my colossal conceit, I didn't take into account,' he freely owned, 'was that, far from falling in love with *me*, you should show a preference for someone else.'

Having learned a good deal more of Thane since she had worked for him, Joss did not consider him conceited at all. But, 'Khalil?' she queried.

'For one,' he replied.

'Who else?' she questioned in surprise. 'I haven't . . .'

'Chad Woollams, for another,' he told her astonishingly.

'Chad Woollams!'

'You can't be more surprised than I was.'

'But you'd no cause!'

'There was no cause either why I should feel so irritated when Woollams tried to flirt with you under my nose.'

'But you were—irritated?'

'Greatly,' he replied. 'As, too, I was mightily irritated to hear him inviting you out to lunch.'

Casting her mind back, 'That was the day you and I went to lunch with Yazid Rashwan,' she remembered—and was again incredulous at Thane's reply.

'I'd no intention of taking you with me that day,' he confessed. 'Only when it looked as though you might be lunching with Woollams did it occur to me that I had every need of you myself.'

'I was never intended to be at that lunch... You were—jealous!' she exclaimed, thunderstruck. 'That far back, you were...' Just as she found it impossible to believe, by the same token she could not finish.

'That far back I was denying that I was anything of the kind,' he told her with rueful charm. 'That far back I was getting so tangled up about you, I was denying every truth about the emotions battering at me but which were insisting on trying to get through.'

'What sort of emotions?' Joss just had to ask, and as Thane bent his head to her she was kissed so long and so thoroughly that she forgot her question.

'I've an idea I shouldn't have done that,' he teased as he looked down into her flushed face, and, although she had not raised any objection, he pulled back from her and asked, 'Where were we?' Helplessly, Joss shook her head. Thane laughed and pulled her close to him again. 'Oh, dear heaven, how I love you,' he told her, and his voice sounded gravelly in his throat.

'I love you too,' Joss whispered, gazing at him in wonder at all that was happening. 'I think we were talking about jealousy,' she remembered.

'Ah, yes,' Thane took up, cradling her to him. 'Jealousy, and how I was denying its existence even though there were countless instances when it was staring me in the face.'

'Countless?'

'Apart from Woollams, I was having to do battle against the green-eyed monster when Rashwan junior phoned me to ask for your address.'

'That was when I first arrived in Alexandria and you booked me into a hotel?' Joss queried.

'And I was sure I didn't give a damn who knew which hotel you were staying in—which of course was why I was as mad as hell when, with there being no reason in the world for me to phone you, I did so and found the line to your room was busy.'

'You rang back,' Joss remembered, 'and demanded to know if I was dining with Khalil, and I thought it would please you to know that I wasn't dining with him...'

'And it did, of course, and I didn't like that either— that it should please me. I, my dear love,' he told her, 'was starting to get very mixed up about you.'

'It never showed,' she said warmly, and was gently kissed.

'I apologise wholeheartedly now, for every time I've ever been the least bit disagreeable to you,' Thane said handsomely, 'but, in my defence, nothing like this has ever happened to me before—and I not only did not trust it, did not want it, but did not want to believe it either.'

'Was it so bad?' she teased, and was kissed again for her sauce.

'Murder,' Thane smiled. 'I barely knew you that afternoon you went to that museum with Khalil Rashwan, yet, when I'd returned to work and you hadn't,

I discovered that I was concentrating more on listening for your footsteps than I was on the job in hand.'

'Truly?' she gasped in astonishment.

'Truly,' he replied, and added, 'I went home that night, and when I'd determined that you were nothing to me, what do I do but damn well dream of you? You, my little love, have given me one hell of a time!'

'Should I be sorry?' she smiled.

'Yes, you should!' he retorted. 'How dare you ruin my peace of mind by telling me not once, but twice, that you quite liked Khalil Rashwan?'

The second time was recently, when Thane had come to her room in fact, Joss remembered. 'When was the first time?' she enquired.

'Heartless woman, how can you have forgotten?' he charged mock-severely—then reminded her, 'It was more or less in the same breath as you categorically stated that you didn't even like me—much less fancy me.'

'Oh, Thane,' cried Joss, instantly contrite. 'Did I hurt your feelings?'

'Not so much,' he said cheerfully, 'because you also told me that you'd no intention of going to bed with him.'

'Oh!' she exclaimed suddenly. 'That was the night you kissed me and then had the nerve to tell me that I'd turn on without such niceties as having a liking for a man.'

'You've so much to forgive me for,' Thane said quietly. 'I didn't know then, of course, that you had never—so to speak—turned on for any man to the extent I accused you of.' Gently then he kissed her.

'You—kissed me like that—the night...'

'And regained my senses on Saturday morning to realise that I didn't at all like the hold one certain most beautiful blonde had on me.'

'Oh, Thane!' Joss sighed, but, recalling how grumpy he'd been the next time she'd seen him, 'So that's why...'

'Exactly,' he cut in, as if he was not liking the memory of the grim person he had been that Saturday morning. 'But to get back to the previous evening, that was the night that I discovered you didn't sleep around. Forgive the male chauvinist in me, my love,' he said softly, 'but I felt so good to know that—that it just seemed entirely natural that I should take you in my arms.'

By then Joss was ready to forgive him anything. 'That was Friday, the night you came to tell me we were going to Luxor,' she said dreamily.

'That was the night I returned from England and, when I could have easily sent a messenger to tell you to pack a case, while still denying that I'd missed you in the two days I'd been away, I found that I just had to come in person.'

'Because you'd missed me!'

Thane grinned, kissed her lightly on the nose, then confessed, 'That wasn't the only time, my dear one,' and, when she looked at him expectantly, 'I was refusing to believe it, of course, but—remember driving with me to Cairo last Monday?'

'Of course,' she replied. 'Though I can't say that—although I took a few notes—you needed me along on that trip.'

'I didn't—from a work point of view,' Thane told her, and at her look of surprise, 'But dammit, woman, I'd just spent an entire weekend not seeing you and—even if I wasn't admitting it—I'd missed you, and wanted a few hours in your company.'

'Oh—if I'm dreaming, never wake me up!' sighed Joss.

'You're not dreaming, beloved,' he breathed tenderly, and held her against his heart.

For some minutes they sat close in each other's arms and, after having been through a welter of unhappiness when she had flown away from him in Luxor, she asked, 'When did you know for sure that—about your feelings, for me?'

'You mean when did I pull my head out of the sand and finally admit that I love and adore you?' Thane smiled. Then, looking down into her lovely shining velvety eyes, 'Yesterday,' he told her, going on, 'Having told you I'd no need of you and that you could do as much sightseeing as you wanted, I was suddenly bedevilled by the notion that I wanted to show you the sights myself.'

'You!'

'Me,' he replied. 'Which was why I hot-footed it down to reception and waited for you to come out of the lift.'

'You were waiting...!' she began, flabbergasted. 'You were making an enquiry; you might have missed seeing me. You...'

'No chance,' he told her. 'I spotted you the moment those lift doors opened—and pretended I hadn't.' Joss was staring at him in amazement when, his expression going suddenly serious he went on, 'We were in the bazaar, and you were looking at that rug. You said, "It's beautiful," and as I looked at you I knew then that I'd never felt happier in my entire life, and that I was enjoying every moment of my time with you. It was then I could no longer escape the truth. The truth being that, having more or less told you at the outset not to fall in love with me—I'd fallen totally and irrevocably in love with you.'

'Oh, Thane!' Joss sighed ecstatically.

'I knew then, dear heart, why I'd felt such a dreadful pang when I'd had to leave you to fly to England on Wednesday.'

'You'd—er—been going to leave me the safe key,' she whispered inconsequentially.

'Can you wonder, with you, with parting from you so much in my head, that I should forget it?' he murmured. 'Though it wasn't until yesterday, Sunday, that I understood what had motivated my actions in taking you protectively to my apartment on your first night in Egypt, or accepted that jealousy was behind my immediately setting about finding you an apartment without a phone when you told me that Khalil Rashwan was in the habit of ringing you at your hotel of an evening.'

'Really? But—but I distinctly remember you asking me if he still rang me every evening.' Suddenly she was looking astounded. 'You—knew *then* that I didn't have a phone!'

Thane refused to look abashed. 'That didn't stop him ringing you at the office, did it! Nor me from trying to tell you how—with him being Yazid's son—I needed to know everything. I afterwards wondered who I was trying the hardest to convince—you, or myself.'

'You knew it was yourself—yesterday?' asked Joss, getting to like this feeling that Thane really, really did love her.

Gently he stroked his fingers down the sides of her face. 'Oh, yes, my darling,' he breathed. 'I knew as we took that rug to be air-freighted that, having never experienced such inner joy at being with another person, I never wanted that day to end.' He smiled tenderly as he added, 'What better way to prolong it than to take you to lunch?'

Blissfully, Joss sighed again. 'And then to Karnak,' she murmured.

'And in the evening, back to Karnak for the Son et Lumière.'

'It was all so beautiful, so heavenly,' she whispered.

'Only I and my giant-sized jealousy have to go and ruin everything when, while in the room next to yours, I hear Khalil Rashwan's voice as I'm dressing.'

'You—er—came in pretty quickly,' Joss recalled.

'And for my sins had my jealousy go into overdrive to see some other man dare to take you in his arms. Oh, my dear, dear love, are you ever going to forgive me for my words and actions after that?'

'For—hitting Khalil?'

'Huh!' scorned Thane. 'He had it coming! No, my darling, for not merely accusing you of giving me the green light all day—wishful thinking on my part—but for damn near seducing you, and then for going on to accuse you of wanton behaviour with Khalil Rashwan. Topping it all—by dismissing you.'

'Er—why did you?' she asked quietly.

'Dismiss you?'

She shook her head. 'Any of it?' she replied, and basked in the glow of his tender expression.

'I'd lost my head over you, dear love,' he told her gently. 'In the first instance, I just went over the top from rage at Khalil Rashwan's daring to lay a hand on you. Then, when in anger I took you in my arms, I started to lose control completely. But for your having a last moment of reservation in our lovemaking, I should have been lost,' he murmured gently. 'But when you did suffer a moment of—hesitation, it gave a chance for a little sense to penetrate my mind. I wasn't sure what the hell it was that I wanted any more, sweet love,' he breathed. 'But even in my tangled brain patterns, I somehow just seemed to know that it couldn't be that I should want to take you in anger.'

'You were gentle then,' Joss reminded him quietly.

'In that moment of a stray strand of sense returning, I was scared,' Thane told her.

'Scared—you?'

'Believe it,' he smiled. 'I wanted you—dear heaven, how I wanted you! Which was why I had to get you to hide your body from me. But even though you'd covered yourself up, the memory of your beauty was still haunting me. I was scared, Joss, that I might yet go on to make you mine. I needed some help.'

'Ah!' she exclaimed as she recalled how, given that she had known a belated moment's shyness, she would not have stopped him had he not torn himself away from her. 'You needed me angry, not—er—compliant.'

He nodded in agreement that she had worked it out correctly. 'I had to accuse you of ruining my work, of being wanton, but then, while still in panic and desperately wanting you, I started to fear that in the gentleness—which you'd spotted—I might have revealed my love for you. I confess, Joss, my normal logical thinking processes had totally deserted me when I decided that you would soon know I certainly had no love for you—were I to dismiss you.'

'Oh, Thane, my poor darling!' Joss crooned, able then to see how very desperate he must have been.

'You forgive me?' he asked.

'Of course,' she smiled, and reached up and kissed him, and all was silent in the room as they shared the solace of each other's lips.

'Did I ever tell you that I think you're truly beautiful, adorable, and that I love you with all the heart that's in me?' Thane questioned softly as their kiss broke.

Joss smiled up at him. 'I don't think so,' she laughed, then thought to question, 'If you were so set on my *not* knowing how you—er—felt about me, what...'

'What made me decide to tell you after all?'

She nodded. 'You said I'd given you a fright, lighting out the way I did. Was it that that——?'

'I'd decided before that to try and find out how things were with you and if I stood a chance,' Thane butted in. 'When I left you—your room, I went charging out of the hotel, seriously needing to get my head together. I must have walked miles,' he went on, 'before I suddenly found I was starting to get hooked on the notion that you—to have been the way you had with me—might, dare I hope, have some feeling for me. Could it be—that I had no need to hide how I felt about you? I grabbed a taxi as soon as I could and, in a sweat, returned to the hotel to find you.'

'But I wasn't there.'

'That was when the nightmare really began,' he smiled, then grinned and added, 'You started to get to me way back, Miss Harding, do you know that?'

'I'm sure it never showed, Mr Addison,' she beamed, and felt she wouldn't have been human if she hadn't asked, 'When exactly?'

'You're such a delight to me,' he said softly, and took time out to place a kiss on her nose, before he went on to reveal, 'I was driving to Alexandria with you—that day you arrived in Egypt when, out on your feet, your head began to droop until finally it landed on my shoulder. I was about to tell you in no uncertain terms to sit up straight, when suddenly I glanced at you—and the words just wouldn't come. Despite myself,' he owned, 'I found I was taken by the sleeping, innocent and vulnerable look of you, and—against all my inner convictions, and all before I know it—I discovered that instead of dropping you off at a hotel, which is what I fully meant to do, I'd—can you believe it?—driven you to my apartment. Is it any wonder,' he asked, 'that I was not only very much annoyed with myself, but with you too?'

'I wasn't liking you very much that night,' Joss smiled in understatement when she recalled how infuriated he had made her.

Thane smiled too, but his expression had gone serious as he began, 'My darling, I've explained everything I have because, after the way I've behaved to you, I've felt that you've needed to know how it is with me, and the depth of my love for you. But now, beloved little Joss, can I ask you to tell me when you knew that you—loved me?'

It seemed incredible to her that Thane should need reassurance that she truly did love him, and need to know when. But willingly she obliged. 'I knew for certain that I was in love with you the night we went to dine at Yazid Rashwan's home.'

'The night I was such an unbearable swine to you?'

'My sentiments exactly.' Joss grinned, was kissed for her trouble, but was then allowed to resume. 'We'd been driven back to our hotel, and I was going up in the lift on my own when, in the middle of mutinying against you, I suddenly realised why it was that your changes of mood could so affect my mood.'

'Er—had it been coming on before then?' he fished openly.

'What can I tell you?' she laughed. 'It was all there in the fact that when I realised that agreement over that contract had been reached I wanted, without knowing why, to kiss you.' On impulse she stretched up and kissed him. 'Congratulations,' she murmured, and when he looked adoringly at her she coughed to clear a suddenly emotionally dry throat, and went on, 'I've since realised, of course, that when I was telling you that not only did I not like you but that also neither did I fancy you, I was deluding myself as much as you. Even then I think I was loving you more than hating you. But,' she came to a smiling end, 'if I'm honest, I think love for you must have started to stir in me on that very night you took me to your apartment.'

Joss laughed again when, in utter bliss at being in his arms, and the belief that he really did love her starting to firmly cement, Thane pressed, 'I want you to be honest.'

She began to feel even more secure in his love as she realised that, just as she had wanted to know all about the emotions that had raged in him about her, so it seemed that he wanted to know all about her feelings for him.

'Well, one of my reactions that night was to fight against the impulse to tell you what you could do with your job,' she revealed—but then owned, 'Though I've since wondered if I was deceiving myself when I decided that I'd stay just to show you, and stay because I hadn't seen the Pyramids yet—because now I wonder, did I stay because even then you had that something "special" for me?'

Thane looked deeply into her eyes, then, lowering his head, he kissed her long and satisfyingly. Then, pulling back, he moved her until they were both standing. Then, 'Talking of pyramids, my love,' he said tenderly, and added mysteriously, 'If my geography's right...' and took her with him to the sliding door.

He was holding her to him with one arm as he slid the door back and, with Joss entirely unprotesting, he took her out on to the balcony. Somewhere a cockerel crowed, and her glance went from the tall eucalyptus tree to her left to the faint pink in the dawn sky. Then Thane was moving to the back of her and was turning her to look to her right.

'Thane!' she gasped, and just could not believe it. Then, 'Thane!' she cried again in complete and utter wonderment. For there, so close that she felt she could almost touch them, were the three Pyramids of Giza! She opened her mouth again, but so absolutely astounded was she that no sound came.

Totally surprised and much in awe of the two large Pyramids with a smaller one to the left-hand side, all shrouded in the early morning mist but clearly discernible for all that, Joss remained completely speechless.

How long she stood like that she had no idea. But, safe in the haven of Thane's arms, she at last gave a sigh of utter contentment, and let her head rest on his shoulder.

That was when Thane came to her side and half turned her to face him. In sublime happiness she raised her eyes to his, and at the warmth in his eyes her heart started racing anew, and he cupped her face in his hands.

Then, after taking a deep breath, 'My dearest Joss,' he began quietly, 'because I travel all over the globe and am often away from England for months at a time, I've put all thoughts of marrying out of my head.' Her eyes were large in her face as wordlessly, her heart not merely racing but sprinting wildly, she stared up at him. 'Up until now, I've been quite content, indeed, have enjoyed my bachelor status,' he continued, 'and have always known that my job meant more to me than marriage. But that, my own, was before I met and fell so heart and soul in love with you.' He paused, and taking a very deep breath—with the Pyramids forming a backcloth— he watched every expression in her face, then said, 'So what I need to know now, my heart, given that without you nothing has any meaning any more, is—will you marry me—*please*?'

Her heart gave a further burst of energetic energy, and Joss swallowed hard. She felt so near to emotional, happy tears, but looking at Thane, loving him and, unbelievably, observing from his tense expression that he seemed to be in some doubt about her answer, she put a gentle hand to the side of his face. And then she smiled.

'Since you ask so nicely,' she whispered chokily, her feelings for him all there in her look, 'yes, I will.'

'My love!' he breathed, and with a heartfelt sigh he gathered her into his arms.

Six exciting series for you every month... from Harlequin

HARLEQUIN
American Romance®
Harlequin celebrates the American woman...

...by offering you romance stories written about American women, by American women for American women. This series offers you contemporary romances uniquely North American in flavor and appeal.

HARLEQUIN
Temptation®

Passionate stories for today's woman

An exciting series of sensual, mature stories of love...dilemmas, choices, resolutions... all contemporary issues dealt with in a true-to-life fashion by some of your favorite authors.

Harlequin Intrigue®
Because romance can be quite an adventure

Harlequin Intrigue, an innovative series that blends the romance you expect... with the unexpected. Each story has an added element of intrigue that provides a new twist to the Harlequin tradition of romance excellence.

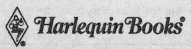

Harlequin Books®

PROD-A-2R

HARLEQUIN
Romance®

Delight in the exotic yet innocent love stories of
Harlequin Romance.

Be whisked away to dazzling international capitals ... or
quaint European villages.

Experience the joys of falling in love ... for the first
time, the best time!

Six new titles every month for your
reading enjoyment!